"Go to sleep," and Abigail closed her eyes at last. *"The morning will be here soon."*

He buried his face in her hair, his fingers itching to bury themselves in the thick richness, pulling her head back for his kiss.

He wanted to do other things, too. He'd known she needed the comfort of a warm body after she woke from her nightmare, and he couldn't turn away from that need. So he'd created his own hell.

His body wanted the woman in his arms. His head told him Abigail didn't want him, she simply wanted some comfort. And yet he remembered the desire he'd seen in her eyes.

Elijah gritted his teeth. *Go to sleep,* he counseled himself. No matter how much he wanted to make love to Abigail, he couldn't. He had to keep his hands to himself.

But…

Sleep was a long time in coming.

Dear Reader,

It's no surprise that Intimate Moments is *the* place to go when
you want the best mix of excitement and romance, and it's authors
like Sharon Sala who have earned the line that reputation. Now,
with *Ryder's Wife*, Sharon begins her first Intimate Moments
miniseries, THE JUSTICE WAY. The three Justice brothers
are men with a capital M—and they're about to fall in love
with a capital L. This month join Ryder as he marries heiress
Casey Ruban for reasons of convenience and stays around for
love.

Popular Beverly Barton is writing in the miniseries vein, too, with
A Man Like Morgan Kane, the latest in THE PROTECTORS.
Beverly knows how to steam up a romance, that's for sure! In
Wife, Mother...Lover? Sally Tyler Hayes spins a poignant tale
of a father, a family and the woman who gives them all their
second chance at happiness—and love. *Reilly's Return* also
marks Amelia Autin's return. This is a wonderfully suspenseful
tale about a hero who had to fake his own death to protect the
woman he loved—and what happens when she suddenly finds out
he's really still alive. In *Temporary Marriage*, Leann Harris takes
us to the jungles of South America for a tale of a sham marriage
that leads to a very real honeymoon. Finally, Dani Criss is back
with *For Kaitlyn's Sake*, a reunion story with all the passion you
could wish for.

Let all six of these terrific books keep you warm as the winter
nights grow colder, and come back next month for even more of
the most excitingly romantic reading around, right here in
Silhouette Intimate Moments.

Yours,

Leslie Wainger

Leslie J. Wainger
Senior Editor and Editorial Coordinator

Please address questions and book requests to:
Silhouette Reader Service
U.S.: 3010 Walden Ave., P.O. Box 1325, Buffalo, NY 14269
Canadian: P.O. Box 609, Fort Erie, Ont. L2A 5X3

TEMPORARY MARRIAGE

LEANN HARRIS

Published by Silhouette Books

America's Publisher of Contemporary Romance

If you purchased this book without a cover you should be aware that this book is stolen property. It was reported as "unsold and destroyed" to the publisher, and neither the author nor the publisher has received any payment for this "stripped book."

 SILHOUETTE BOOKS

ISBN 0-373-07821-8

TEMPORARY MARRIAGE

Copyright © 1997 by Barbara M. Harrison

All rights reserved. Except for use in any review, the reproduction or utilization of this work in whole or in part in any form by any electronic, mechanical or other means, now known or hereafter invented, including xerography, photocopying and recording, or in any information storage or retrieval system, is forbidden without the written permission of the editorial office, Silhouette Books, 300 East 42nd Street, New York, NY 10017 U.S.A.

All characters in this book have no existence outside the imagination of the author and have no relation whatsoever to anyone bearing the same name or names. They are not even distantly inspired by any individual known or unknown to the author, and all incidents are pure invention.

This edition published by arrangement with Harlequin Books S.A.

® and TM are trademarks of Harlequin Books S.A., used under license. Trademarks indicated with ® are registered in the United States Patent and Trademark Office, the Canadian Trade Marks Office and in other countries.

Printed in U.S.A.

LEANN HARRIS

When Leann Harris first met her husband in college, she never dreamed she would marry him. After all, he was getting a Ph.D. in the one science she'd managed to avoid—physics! So much for first impressions. They have been happily married for twenty-one years. After graduating from the University of Texas at Austin, Leann taught math and science to deaf high school students until the birth of her first child. It wasn't until her youngest child started school that Leann decided to fulfill a lifelong dream and began writing. She presently lives in Plano, Texas, with her husband and two children.

My deepest thanks to Lieutenant Davis for his insight on the CIA, and Judy Christenberry, who is the best of friends. And to the ladies of Friday morning, thanks.

Chapter 1

Abigail McGee stifled a yawn as she pulled her aged VW van to a halt in front of her house. She'd been up for the last thirty hours, helping to deliver Alice Stanford's first baby, and now both mother and baby were doing fine. A satisfied smile curved Abigail's mouth. She'd been right to become a nurse-midwife. Although it was a fairly new concept for modern medicine, in the Appalachian mountains, midwifery had never gone out of style.

After turning off the engine, she grabbed her medical bag and slid out of the car. The early pre-dawn sky was overcast and the air crisp and cold. Abigail filled her lungs with the invigorating smells of her mountain home. Autumn was in the air.

When she landed this job, Abigail had felt immediately at home in the mountains and hollers of this part of Kentucky. Of course, nothing could've been farther away from the steamy jungles of Brazil where she'd grown up, but as far as she was concerned, this depressed area was heaven.

She climbed the porch steps and came to an abrupt halt on the second-to-last step. Sitting in one of the porch chairs was a young, stunningly handsome man. She'd never seen him before, but that didn't mean a thing. Several times over the last eighteen months, a stranger had shown up on her porch, asking for help for his pregnant wife, sister or girlfriend.

She silently groaned. At this moment, she was too tired to deal with another birth.

"How far along is your wife?" Abigail asked the man.

He gave her a blank look. "What?"

"How far apart are your wife's contractions?"

His eyes narrowed as he studied her. "I'm not here in connection with your job. I don't have a wife, and nobody I know is expecting."

That set her back. "If you don't need a midwife, then why are you here?"

His gaze scanned the woods surrounding her house. "Can we go inside and talk?" His voice was rough and low, and the visions his request brought to mind had nothing to do with talking.

Warning bells sounded in her head. This stranger had yet to identify himself and wanted her to invite him into her house. She shook her head, then said, "Why don't you tell me what you want."

He gave her a measuring look. "All right." He nodded to the chair beside him. "Would you like a seat?"

She didn't want to get near him. Already all her nerves were humming. Getting closer would only make things worse. "I'll stand here if you don't mind."

He shrugged, but the twinkle in his eyes left the impression that he admired her caution. Standing, he walked to the side of the porch and rested his hip on the handrail. "I need your help, Ms. McGee."

She gave him a blank look. "If you don't have a wife, and nobody you know is pregnant, why do you need my services?"

"You are the daughter of missionaries David and Lisa McGee, aren't you?"

If he'd hit her with a board, she couldn't have been more surprised. "Yes, those are my parents."

"And they spent time in the jungles of the Amazon Basin, teaching reading and writing to the natives."

"Yes. They learned the native language, translated it into a written form, then taught the natives to read and write." She didn't tell him that her parents had been dead for the last five years. "What is it you want, Mr.—" He still had not introduced himself.

He smiled at her. It was a well-practiced move that probably served him well, putting people off their guard and easing tense situations. "Kendrick, Elijah."

"Apparently my folks weren't the only ones who depended on the Bible for the name of their child." Her teasing comment didn't go over well. His gaze hardened and his lips compressed into a thin line.

"Why are you here, Mr. Kendrick?" she asked, to ease over the awkward moment.

"I need your help."

"Again, if you don't have a wife—"

"That's not the kind of help I need."

His comment completely puzzled her. "Then, why

are you here?'' she asked for the third time, impatiently.

He rubbed his chin, then rolled his shoulders. "Ms. McGee, yesterday, a United States government plane went down in northern Brazil near Boa Vista on the Branco River, which as you know is one of the branches of the Amazon. It's a remote area, and the rescue operation needs liaison between the natives and the government team."

"Why does the government need a go-between?"

He flushed. "It appears things are rocky between the Brazilian officials and the tribe. Something to do with modernization and cutting down the rain forest."

Abigail could well imagine the rift between the natives and government.

"The area of the jungle where your parents lived is the last known location we have for the plane. The regional government told us of the problem they had and recommended we contact you. I want you to come with me and help me get the local tribe's cooperation to guide me to the downed plane."

Abigail felt the blood drain from her face. Her legs suddenly became like gelatin, and she sat down heavily on the top step. Of all the things she didn't want to do, visiting the area of her youth was top on the list. Oh, she didn't have a problem with the land or people. What she had a problem with was facing the memories of her parents.

"I have patients in these mountains, Mr. Kendrick, who can't go without my help."

"There's a nurse on her way now to care for your patients while you're gone."

He seemed to think he had the answer to her objection.

"Obviously, you don't understand much about the people of this region, Mr. Kendrick. Only now are they beginning to trust me. I don't know how they would react to a replacement nurse."

He walked over to where she sat and squatted down beside her. "I think if it's explained to your patients why you had to leave, they might accept a substitute. How many births are you expecting over the next month?"

Her mind reviewed all her patients and couldn't come up with a single woman who was due before the end of October, six weeks away. "None."

After pinning her with a probing stare, he asked, "Then, what's the problem, Ms. McGee?"

Abigail glanced away into the soothing quietness of the surrounding forest, fighting for her composure.

"The problem, Mr. Kendrick, is that I don't want to go." She folded her arms across her chest and met his gaze. She felt childish and petty, but that couldn't be helped.

He wasn't put off by her bad attitude. "And why is that?"

Abigail stared at the handsome man in front of her. Here was a total stranger asking her highly personal questions and expecting an answer. Well, she had no intention of telling him of her private demons. She stood and looked down at him. "I guess I've adopted some of the customs of this region, Mr. Kendrick. My reasons are private and I don't care to divulge them."

Her answer went over like a lead balloon. Mr. Kendrick slowly stood. She had to crane her head back to continue to keep him in view. His expression was hard as stone, and he reminded her of an avenging angel rising above her.

"You're the only hope those people—ten people—have of surviving, Ms. McGee."

Why didn't he just take out his gun—something about the man said he had one—and shoot her? It probably would have been less painful. If she turned him down, could she live with the fact that she was probably one of the only individuals outside the river basin who could save those people?

She eyed the man above her. "You don't play fair, do you, Mr. Kendrick."

His mouth curved into a sensuous smile that took her breath away. "Not playing fair is one of my specialties, Ms. McGee."

Of that she had no doubt. In the center of her chest, she felt a sinking feeling, a warning that she was going to cooperate with this man. "Do you have any ID with you?" If she couldn't deny him, at least she could satisfy herself that he was telling the truth.

He reached into his back pocket, pulled out his wallet, opened it, then handed it to her. Abigail took the wallet from his hand and glanced down at the ID. The picture was a good likeness of the man and proclaimed him an agent of the CIA.

She looked up, surprised. "You're with the CIA?" There was a strangled tone in her voice.

He nodded.

"Was this a CIA plane that went down?"

She saw his stance stiffen, and a guarded look entered his eyes. "No, it wasn't."

There was something here he wasn't telling her. She felt it in her bones. She pushed aside her misgivings and looked back at his identification.

Across from the government ID was his Virginia driver's license, giving his vital statistics. He was born 11/2/61, and was six foot four and two hundred and ten pounds. He had brown hair and brown eyes. Unfortunately, that bland description didn't tell half the story of the golden, mesmerizing effect of his eyes or the way his hair fell over his forehead.

"Are you satisfied?" he asked.

A tide of red rushed up her neck. She felt like a fool when she handed the wallet back to him. "No."

"I've got my company badge I wear in the building when I'm on the job. Would you like to see it?"

She held out her hand, indicating that she wanted to see his CIA badge. He pulled the ID from his shirt pocket. Again, the likeness on the ID didn't capture the virility of the man. At the bottom of the badge was a bar code. She glanced up at him.

"That's what I use to access certain areas of the building. It's for security."

"Oh."

She handed back the ID. He slipped it into his pocket.

"What's the number of the CIA?" she asked. His story was just too unbelievable. She couldn't swallow his story without some other sort of proof. "I'd like to check you out, Mr. Kendrick."

"You don't believe me?" He sounded amazed that she wouldn't believe him.

"You've got to admit that your story is pretty far-fetched. Besides, it's just common sense to be careful in this day and age."

He rattled off the number. "Ask for my boss, Neil Teatly."

She silently repeated the number to herself. She walked around him toward the door. He followed. Pausing after opening the screen, she looked at him, hoping he'd read from her expression that she didn't want him to follow her inside. "I shouldn't be more than five minutes."

He nodded. "Tell Neil hello for me."

She scowled at him, then closed the wooden door in his face. She hurried to the kitchen phone and punched in the number he'd given her. On the second ring, the phone was picked up and the receptionist identified the number as CIA headquarters. A moment later she was connected with Neil Teatly.

"Ah, Miss McGee, I assume you're calling about Elijah."

From the man's response, he knew about Mr. Kendrick's visit. "Yes, I wanted to check out his story. It's rather wild."

"That was a smart move, Miss McGee. What would you like to know?"

"I just wanted to make sure Mr. Kendrick's story is true."

"Yes, indeed, the story about the downed plane is true. There were ten people on that plane, and one of our agents was carrying some sensitive information that we need. You, Miss McGee, are our best hope of saving those people."

Secret documents. It all made sense to her.

"And retrieving your information," she added.

He laughed. "You're an observant woman. You'll be more than a challenge for Elijah."

Abigail didn't care for his comment. After thanking him for the information, she hung up. Taking a deep breath, she focused on the front door, considering the individual on the other side. Apparently, the man on her porch was on the level, which meant that she was going to have to face this situation.

She leaned against the doorjamb, rested her head on the wood and took another deep breath. Of all the places on earth, the Amazon jungle was the last place she wanted to go, because it would call up demons that she had been able to ignore until now. And heaven knew she didn't want to deal with those issues—at least not in this lifetime.

Although she wanted to tell Mr. Kendrick to take a flying leap, she couldn't in good conscience disregard the lives at stake. Fate had chosen to involve her.

Abby felt like she was flying down a deep slide and there was nothing she could do to stop her downward momentum. She considered leaving Mr. Kendrick out on the porch cooling his heels, but there was something about the man that told her he wouldn't allow that to happen.

She crossed the room and opened the door. He was sitting in the same chair he'd originally occupied. He glanced up, and his mouth curved up into a heart-stopping, soul-shattering smile. Apparently, he knew what she'd found out.

"You satisfied?" he asked, his tone smug.

"No, Mr. Kendrick, I'm not."

That wiped the grin off his face. "Wasn't Neil there?"

"He was there."

His eyes narrowed. "Then, what's the problem?"

"The problem?" she repeated, exasperated with the situation. "The problem is a stranger shows up on my porch, then asks me to leave my patients and go with him to the Amazon."

Leaning forward, he said, "I've already told you who I am and what I need."

"I've got people here who need me."

"I need you more."

His words, like a hot brand, sizzled their heat into her brain.

"If you're worried about a substitute, I told you there's one on the way right now. She should be here any minute."

She opened her mouth to argue with him again that her patients needed her and a substitute would be looked at suspiciously. But the needs of the plane passengers tugged at her heart, and she closed her mouth. No matter how she wanted to ignore Mr. Kendrick, the man needed her knowledge of the region, needed her connection to the tribe.

"I'm willing to compensate you for your time, Ms. McGee, if that's the sticking point."

His comment hit her with the force of an open-handed slap. "You think it's a matter of money, Mr. Kendrick?" Her voice shook with outrage.

"With most people it is." His tone was even and sure, as if stating the obvious didn't need any emphasis.

"Well, I'm not most people," she shot back, her outrage simmering.

"Forgive my assumption. I'm used to dealing with a lot of different people, from different countries, and the common thread among them is monetary. They want to be compensated for their work with the CIA."

She thought about his explanation. It made sense, and perhaps she was being a bit too thin-skinned about the situation.

"I don't know how friendly the natives will be," she tried to explain. "The first time my family was there, they didn't trust us. The second time my folks went back, they achieved a certain amount of success.''

''What I need is you, Abigail.''

She wished he'd stop saying that. It was wreaking havoc with her emotions. Walking out onto the porch, she stared off into the dense trees surrounding her house. ''All right, Mr. Kendrick. I'll go.''

She faced him. He nodded.

''Go pack what you need. When the nurse gets here I'll send her in.''

Without another word or a glance in his direction, she walked into the house and closed the door behind her, wishing she could close out her memories as easily.

Elijah stared at the closed door, then the corner of his mouth lifted in a ghost of a smile. Well, his meeting with Abigail McGee certainly had been eventful. He'd been prepared to get down and dirty with his pressure on her to get her cooperation. Amazingly, with a minimum of fuss, she had agreed to help.

He shook his head and stared out into the pines surrounding the house. Abigail McGee was perfect for this situation.

When the former head of East German counterintelligence had approached their agent in Argentina, willing to sell out a mole at the CIA and provide proof of his activities, Elijah had been able to set up this buy of documents. But the private jet carrying the agent—Elijah's friend—and the papers bought from the East German had disappeared from the radar screen early yesterday evening. After several hours of scrambling, the local authorities had confessed that their relationship with the tribe in the area of the downed plane was strained due to the modernization and deforestation of the jungle that had taken place over the past few years. When Elijah pressed them, they had given him Abigail's name. She might be able to help, they informed him, since her parents had worked with the tribe.

He sat down. He thought convincing her would've been harder than it proved to be. But after voicing her initial objection, she had come quickly around to his point of view. Her only prerequisite had been to find a replacement nurse, which he had already anticipated.

What had surprised him the most about his encounter with Abigail was how his body had reacted to her. He hadn't experienced such a hormone rush since he was fifteen and Cecilia Ward had moved in next door to his foster parents. She'd driven him crazy all summer long parading around in her swimsuit. Now, here he was a grown man, and he still hadn't quite known how to handle his sudden burst of testosterone.

At first he'd tried to ignore his reaction, but when that failed, he concentrated on the seriousness of the situation that had brought him to these mountains. That tack had worked, but he still felt somewhat disoriented.

He had to smile as he recalled Abigail's reaction to him. From the initial look on her face, he could tell he wasn't the only one who felt the magnetic currents swirling around them.

He let loose a string of pithy curses. This was not the time to come down with a case of lust. How was he going to handle the next week with her, trekking through the hot jungles of Brazil? The prospect was enough to make him break out in a sweat. And yet, he needed to keep a clear head for his friend's sake as well as for the agency's benefit.

Nothing was going to come from his relationship with Abigail. She was the daughter of missionaries, probably as straitlaced as they came.

Still, something had sparked between them. And no matter how hard he tried, he couldn't ignore that spark. He let loose with another blistering curse. "Terrific, Kendrick," he scolded himself. "For the first time in more than a dozen years, you got an itch and it can't be scratched. Figures."

After latching her suitcase, Abigail paused and glanced at the picture on her dresser. It was of her family, taken shortly before they left the Amazon. She walked across the floor and picked up the frame. The smiles on everyone's faces spoke of the love they had for one another.

"I don't want to do this," she murmured, talking to her memories. Closing her eyes, she threw her head back and took a deep breath. She might not want to do this, but she didn't have a choice.

Shaking off the past, she went to the kitchen and filled her mug with the freshly brewed coffee. She wished she could ignore the man on the porch, but finally admitted to herself she couldn't. She filled a second mug and took it out on the porch.

"Would you like some coffee, Mr. Kendrick?"

His face lit up. "You're an angel," he said, accepting the mug. "I was going through caffeine withdrawal and was about to break down your door and storm the kitchen."

"I know the feeling. I'm useless until I have at least two cups."

She wandered over to the stairs and sat down. She loved this time of the morning when things were fresh and held the promise of a new day. When she was a youngster, the mornings in the jungle were the times she spent with her parents. The heat of the day hadn't arrived and the air had been filled with the sweet and strong fragrance of the wildflowers that surrounded their hut.

A frown creased her brow as she thought of the coming days in the jungle. Since her parents' deaths nearly five years ago, Abigail had tried diligently to avoid thinking about them. It was too painful. Nor had she been able to see why God had allowed such good people to die in a fiery crash.

Her mind shied away from that line of questioning. She'd discovered no answers in the intervening years. After all this time, she was tired of trying.

"How long have you been a midwife?" Elijah asked, drawing her out of her thoughts.

She glanced over her shoulder. "I'm surprised that information wasn't in my file."

When he didn't respond, she looked back at him. His eyebrow arched slightly.

"You probably know what I made in each of my classes."

"A smart man goes into every situation as prepared as he can be."

His answer irritated her. Instead of lashing out at him, she turned her thoughts to the patients she needed to discuss with the new nurse. Caroline Lee had high blood pressure and needed to be monitored for a preeclampsia. Mary Steward was carrying twins, and the nurse needed to keep track of her activities. Mary already had two children, and Abigail was afraid she wouldn't take care of herself and, as a result, would lose the twins. There were other patients, but Mary and Caroline were her main concerns.

Abigail heard the faint sound of a motor. Within minutes, a black Ford parked in front of her house and a woman stepped out. Suddenly Elijah appeared at her side.

"Hello, Sarah," he called out over Abigail's shoulder. He turned to her. "Take ten minutes and fill in Sarah about your patients, then we'll leave." He sounded like a general issuing orders to his troops.

Abigail eyed him. He was tall and handsome, with an air of mystery and danger around him. If she was going to get through this coming encounter with him, she was going to need all the emotional distance she could get.

"Are you used to having your orders obeyed?"

He nodded. "I'll be waiting here."

And that was a perfect summation of her problem.

He was sitting on the porch, a cup of coffee in his hand. Abigail felt his eyes zero in on her.

"How did it go?" he asked.

"As well as could be expected," she answered, coming out of the house. She stopped in front of his chair. "My patients won't be thrilled with the idea of me leaving, but when the situation is explained to them, I hope they'll allow Sarah to help."

He stood, towering over Abigail's five-foot-six frame, making her feel small and womanly. "Are you ready to go?"

"I need my suitcase. It's in the bedroom."

"Don't worry." He took her arm and guided her down the steps. Her skin sizzled at the contact. "I've already taken care of it," he explained as he guided her to his car.

Abigail swallowed hard. She wasn't looking forward to this experience.

Chapter 2

Abigail stared out the airplane window at the mountainous landscape below. Elijah had driven to a private landing strip over the state line in West Virginia. Within an hour of meeting him on her porch, they were in the air.

"Have you had any further information about the crash and the people?" she asked, dreading the discussion.

"A little. The plane went down in the Serra de Apiau Mountains in northwestern Brazil. The authorities have heard nothing from the pilot or plane since it disappeared from the radar screen. We're going to land in Boa Vista. We'll travel to the village where your folks were and see if we can hire natives to guide us through the region."

She remembered Boa Vista. Her parents had taken her there several times to obtain supplies. The memories were bittersweet. "You shouldn't have any trouble hiring help."

His eyes narrowed, and he studied her for several moments. "Have you been to Boa Vista?"

"Several times when I was a kid."

A satisfied look entered his eyes. "I knew you were the perfect person for this job, felt it in my bones. In over ten years of working in this business, you develop a sixth sense. When I first spotted your picture, I knew you were the right person."

There was a wealth of meaning buried in his words that had nothing to do with what he said. She wished she could figure it out, but it seemed the closer they got to Boa Vista, the more her brain shut down. By the time they reached Brazil, she'd be operating only on gut instinct.

But there was one thing that pierced her numbness—awareness of the man beside her. He was dressed in a white shirt and loose tan slacks, appropriate for the region. His brown eyes seemed to sparkle with excitement, as if this adventure was the type of thing he lived for.

"How far from the village did the plane go down?"

"We think somewhere to the northwest. That's where the plane disappeared from the radar screen. There's a homing beacon in the plane that we're counting on to lead us to the crash site."

"So what you're telling me is you really don't know where the plane went down."

He couldn't hold her gaze.

"Do you have any idea how many miles of jungle there are northwest of Boa Vista?"

"A lot."

She burst out laughing. The man didn't have a clue as to what they were facing.

"What are you laughing at?" he growled.

She smothered her laughter and looked at him. This was a man who probably was used to having control over every situation, did all he could to minimize the danger his operatives worked in. "Elijah, do you know the story of Moses when he led the children of Israel out of Egypt?"

"Are you kidding me?" His expression held no mirth.

"No."

"Yeah, I know it."

"He had better odds than you do."

He cursed, then glanced up at her, a dull blush staining his neck. "Sorry."

Her eyes narrowed as she studied him. "You're used to long odds, aren't you?"

"I try to avoid them, but, yeah, I've worked with worse odds."

"But have you worked in the jungle?"

"Not so far, but I've worked in Russia and China. Neither was a picnic."

Without thought, she rested her hand on his arm. Sparks seemed to erupt from the spot. His gaze flew to her hand, then moved to her eyes. Awareness of her as a woman twinkled in his gaze, stealing her breath and making her heart pound. She pulled her hand into her lap. "Wh—" Her tongue seemed to stick to the roof of her mouth. She swallowed and tried again. "When this is over, you tell me if you want to repeat the experience or go back to Russia."

From the look in his eyes, she understood he didn't appreciate her pointing out that this job was going to be tough. "When this is over, Abigail, I'll be more than glad to oblige."

She had the oddest feeling that Elijah's answer had nothing to do with her question.

Elijah folded his arms over his chest. Abigail had just confirmed his worst fears about the situation. That they were facing monumental odds, none in their favor. Even with the homing device, their task was going to be a colossal one.

He glanced at the woman sitting beside him. Her profile was highlighted in the afternoon light. Abigail's hair flamed with the sunlight. Gold-and-red highlights danced within the strands, making him want to plunge his fingers into the mass, to see if it was as warm as it appeared. Her eyes were closed, and from the gentle rise and fall of her chest, he guessed she'd fallen asleep.

He shook his head. He was getting fanciful—and no one at the agency ever called him that. Cold, hard, a first-class SOB, maybe. But not fanciful. He was also the guy who could see the big picture from all the little details. He was the one who had first suspected a mole at the top. Too many operations were going wrong, and information that only an insider would know was getting out and compromising his men.

As far as he could tell, life was much more dangerous now than it was when the East Germans and Russians were still Communist powers. Elijah preferred to deal with the old-timers because they knew the rules and how to play the game. Now all bets were off, and hell was breaking loose all over the place. The information his agent carried was important.

Elijah wanted to catch the slime who'd sold out his country for money. And at this point, the only person who could help him was Abigail McGee. What would she say if she knew that she was helping him nail a traitor? Would she have a problem with that? Well, what she didn't know wouldn't hurt her.

He studied her and was again jolted by a wave of physical awareness. He could close his eyes and simply listen to her breathe and be turned on. Well, he had operated before by ignoring such basic needs. There was that time in East Germany when he went without food for nearly three days as he slipped by guards and citizens. And the time in Siberia when his car had broken down and he'd walked twenty miles in the freezing cold.

Abigail crossed her legs and sighed. Elijah's stomach tightened. He was tempted to reach over, grasp her chin and turn her face toward his so he could kiss her. He felt his fingers begin to itch.

But besides knowing how to ignore his physical needs, Elijah had vowed a long time ago never to be subject to the weakness that had killed his father. A need for a woman, to be loved and to return that feeling, had been his dad's downfall. For Elijah, sex was fine, but anything beyond that was taboo.

Abigail sighed again, reminding him that his needs were making themselves known. He didn't have to sit here and endure this torture. He stood and made his way to the cockpit.

Terrific, he thought sourly. *On the verge of one of the most important missions of his life, and all he could think of was kissing Abigail.*

With the acknowledgement of his condition, Elijah's mood turned even more sour.

* * *

It was dusk when Abigail woke from her nap. The plane was approaching Boa Vista. The thought of seeing the jungle and the city she'd visited as a child brought memories flooding back over her. Tears wet her eyes.

"Is something wrong, Abigail?" Elijah asked.

"No," she answered, shaking her head. "I was just remembering the other times I visited Boa Vista years ago."

"Good memories, I presume."

"Yes, they're good memories. The best time of my life."

Her statement brought his gaze back to her. "Why do you say that?"

"Childhood is the best of times. No worries, no trouble, no thoughts for the future. Living one day at a time, and enjoying every minute to the max."

"Depends on who your parents are."

His bitter statement jerked her out of her reminiscing. From the frigid expression in his eyes, she knew he wouldn't welcome any questions. She opened her mouth to respond, but he glanced back out the window.

Elijah scanned the airport building. Immediately, he spotted a lone man waiting.

A violent curse slipped from his lips, scorching her ears. She silently rebuked him with her gaze.

He shook his head. "Darn. Is that better?"

Abigail bit back a smile. She had the feeling that Elijah didn't often apologize for his behavior. "Thank you," she replied primly.

A dark scowl settled on his features. There was something in his eyes that worried her.

"What's wrong?" she asked, looking out the window to see if she could tell what was disturbing him.

He leaned closer and lowered his voice. "Do you see the man standing in front of the metal hangar?"

It was hard not to spot the lone man. "Yes."

"He's a government official."

Her skin tingled with apprehension. Something wasn't right. "What's wrong with that?"

He turned and studied her. "You want the truth?"

Her heart sank. She had to remember this man was a spy, and spies did whatever it took to win. On the one hand, she didn't want to know what was going on. Yet, she could deal better with the grim truth than a lie. "Yes."

She could see in the depths of his brown eyes that he was deciding how much to tell her. "The local authorities know that the American government is sending a team down here to try and recover the plane."

She didn't respond, knowing that he was saving the unpleasantness for the last.

"Well, as far as they know, the official US rescue group will arrive tomorrow. They're not supposed to know about our early arrival. We're going to go in first and try to recover the sensitive information before it falls into the wrong hands."

"Sensitive information? Secrets that are meant only for CIA eyes?"

He frowned. "Yes."

"And you don't need this guy in your space."

His brow arched. "That's not exactly how I'd describe it."

"I don't doubt it," she grumbled, glancing out of

the window. "So, if no one knows we're coming early, why's he here?"

"That's what I want to know," he replied ominously.

The plane bounced on the runway several times, then came to a stop in front of the building.

"Let me do the talking," he said as he unbuckled his seat belt.

"Why do I feel that's what you're going to want to do the entire time we're here?"

His hand covered hers. "I knew you were a smart lady. This is my arena, and I know how to handle these situations."

She wanted to tell him that the world was in worse shape because of people like him, but she knew it would only make this trip more difficult. "Fine. But I'll want the same cooperation out of you when we get to the village. I know what to expect. I don't believe you do."

He studied her, a gleam of admiration flicking in his eyes. "All right."

He stood, picked up his suitcase, then grabbed the beacon finder from the seat across the isle from where he sat. "Are you ready?"

She scrambled out of her seat and grabbed her bags. "Yes. I'll be right after you."

They made their way to the door. The pilot had opened the door and the ground crew had rolled stairs to the plane. Abigail hurried to catch up with Elijah. He waited at the doorway, then grabbed her hand and pulled her after him.

By the time they got to the bottom, the local official had made his way to the stairway.

"Señor Kendrick, I am Lorenzo Villa. I am with

the Office of the Presidente. I have been assigned to help you in your search for the airplane."

With not so much as a bat of an eyelash did Elijah indicate his displeasure at the official interruption. He took the man's hand and shook it. "It is a pleasure."

"We were not expecting you until tomorrow."

Then why was he here? Abigail wondered.

"I've found our guide," Elijah answered smoothly, "and was able to get here earlier than expected. The others will join us tomorrow as scheduled."

"Ah, your guide is most beautiful." Lorenzo nodded to Abigail. "Would you introduce us?"

Elijah pulled Abigail forward. "This is Abigail McGee. She will act as my liaison with the tribe we need to guide us through the jungle."

"I have heard of the McGees and of their work with the Indians." He took Abigail's hand and placed a kiss on it. "The report on you and your family didn't mention how lovely you are."

"That's because, *señor,* I was fourteen when my parents left and went back to the States."

He nodded with a flirtatious smile before turning back to Elijah. "My car's parked by the terminal door, and I will be happy to take you to a hotel. Please, follow me." He walked around the building to his car. The small green-and-white compact was of indeterminate age, the leather seats clean but worn. After storing their suitcases in the trunk, Elijah and Abigail climbed into the back seat. Elijah's size seemed to dominate the space in the car. Abigail was wedged between the door and his shoulder.

Lorenzo turned and smiled at the couple. "I am still gathering people to go up the river and into the jungle where the plane was reported to have gone down. Tomorrow afternoon, after your compatriots arrive, all will be here and hopefully we will be ready to leave."

Elijah nodded, accepting the delay. His response rang wrong with Abigail. Wouldn't Elijah want to leave as soon as possible? Wasn't that why he'd rushed her out of her home and flown her down here? Then, why was he agreeing with Lorenzo Villa that they would leave tomorrow when the others arrived? She looked into Elijah's eyes and noted the hard, far-away look. His expression made her uncomfortable. Something was wrong, and yet Elijah was going along with this man. Why?

"You will need supplies and *médicos* to go with you, yes?" Lorenzo asked.

In a move that surprised her, Elijah slipped his arm around her shoulders and pulled her close. "Abigail is a nurse practitioner. She can give any emergency medical help that the survivors need. The important thing is that we get to the site as soon as possible."

"Of course." He paused, then glanced in the rear-view mirror. "Will the *señora* need any medical supplies?"

Abigail was still reeling from the feel of Elijah's strong arm around her shoulders, pulling her flush against his body.

"*Señora?*"

Elijah squeezed her closer, silently urging her to respond. "Do you need any supplies?" he softly asked her.

"Yes. If they have some plasma and bandages, that would be a help."

"I will arrange for them to be delivered to your

hotel in the morning. Is there anything else you need?''

Abby dimly heard Elijah ask for the man to arrange for them to get a boat tomorrow morning. Instead, what her mind focused on was the heat of Elijah's body burning into hers. His muscles were like steel, yet warm and inviting, urging her to relax into his strength. He turned to her.

''Can you think of anything else?'' he asked her.

She resisted the urge to yell at him to stop touching her. Years ago another man had pursued her not because of who she was, but because he wanted the prestige that went with dating the daughter of famous missionaries. Here was another man acting as if he cared, when all he wanted was the use of her parents' reputation to ease his way. Keeping her thoughts to herself, she schooled her voice into a cool demeanor. ''No.''

They stopped in front of a brightly lit building. ''Ah, here we are.'' The man in the front seat hopped out. Elijah and Abigail followed him into the building. He waited with them until they signed in. ''I will leave you to rest. I'll be here tomorrow to take you to the river and your boats. Good night.''

Overhead fans moved the moist air, bringing a small amount of relief. They were shown to two second-story rooms that overlooked a peaceful courtyard.

''Are you going to tell me what's going on here, Elijah?'' Abigail asked as Elijah checked the nooks and crannies of her room. ''What you said on the plane and how you acted while we were with Lorenzo didn't exactly jive.''

''I didn't want to alarm him. I wanted him to believe that we were going along with his plan.''

"But we aren't?"

There was a cold light in his eyes. "No."

"What are we going to do?"

"Just let me take care of things, Abigail."

"But—"

"Are you hungry?" Elijah asked her.

From the look on his face, Abigail knew that Elijah wasn't going to say anything more on the subject of Lorenzo. She sighed and considered his offer. She was more sleepy than hungry. She hadn't slept for more than forty hours except to nap on the plane. "I think what I need most is sleep. The last time I slept was Sunday night."

He smiled, a slow, sensuous curving of his lips. "I'm hungry and plan to eat. If you can't sleep, you're more than welcome to join me."

"Thank you, but once my head hits the pillow, I should be out."

"Good night, Abigail," Elijah said as he left her room.

She smiled and nodded. When she closed the door, she rested her forehead on the cool wood. She felt like she'd been put through the wringer. Her emotions were close to the surface and her feelings raw. Memories of her parents and her time in the Amazon when she was young assaulted her. Memories she wasn't ready to face. And they hadn't even left Boa Vista.

Sleep, that's what she needed. That's why her emotions were so volatile. As she climbed into bed, she prayed sleep would restore her balance.

Chapter 3

Elijah sat forward in his balcony chair and viewed the street below. Cars still sped by, but they completely drowned out the sound of the river beyond.

He ran his fingers through his thick brown hair. He'd been doing this job for more than a decade, the last three years from his office in Langley. He'd gotten to the stage of life where it was more interesting to match wits with the opposition from afar than to actually go in and oversee a job.

His bosses had been impressed with his ability to size up an operation and know the best way to further proceed. His uncanny ability had saved more than one operative. And that's why this situation bothered him. It was like a bad case of poison oak; it itched like fire, but he couldn't scratch it.

Throwing his head back, he tried to clear his mind. What popped into his brain was Lorenzo Villa. The man who'd met them had more on his agenda than being helpful to the American government, more specifically the CIA. If the official team was to arrive tomorrow afternoon, what had Lorenzo being doing watching out for them? Had someone in the agency tipped him to be on the lookout?

Elijah felt an unease in his bones. Lorenzo wasn't to be trusted, which meant that he and Abby would have to slip out of the city before they were seen by Lorenzo's watchful eye. This unexpected turn was something he hadn't wanted but had planned for.

He wondered if his operative had gotten together the supplies and boat he'd requested yesterday when they'd talked on the phone. He glanced at his watch. It had been two hours since he'd escorted Abigail to her room. That was all he could give her. He was anxious to start upriver and escape Lorenzo. Besides escaping their tag, the longer the plane went undetected, the slimmer their chances of finding it in the thick jungle. And he wanted to reach the plane before whoever Lorenzo was spying for beat them to the punch.

He slipped from his room and stopped before Abigail's door. It was child's play to pick the lock. He stepped into the darkened room and waited for his eyes to adjust to the dimness. It was easy to spot her, curled on the mattress, her arms wrapped around her pillow. He moved to the bed and covered her mouth with his hand. She jerked awake, her eyes flying open, and a moan rose from her covered mouth.

"Abigail," he harshly whispered. "Abigail, it's me, Elijah."

Her frightened gaze found his face, and her body immediately relaxed. When he was convinced she was awake, he removed his hand.

She clutched the sheet to her chest. "What are you doing in here?" There was a waspish quality to her voice. "Are you trying to scare me to death?"

"It's time to leave."

Her gaze flew to the window. It was dark outside. "But—"

He squatted down and leaned close. "Our government guide has more on his plate than helping us."

"Which means what?" Her voice sounded clearer, as if she was fully awake now.

"Which means I have a bad feeling about Lorenzo. Somebody knows about us and wants us watched. The official team is arriving tomorrow, and we're supposed to be gone by the time they get here."

"Oh." There was an innocent quality in her gaze that spoke of a woman who didn't deal in the shadows.

He sighed, then rubbed the back of his neck. "Abigail, the sensitive information on that plane has to be recovered, and I don't need an audience. Our agent carried a report, and the people named in the report don't want it found. They will go to any length to avoid it surfacing."

"I can't believe—"

He leaned closer. So close that his mouth was a mere breath from hers. They didn't have time to dance this dance, he thought sourly, but he needed her cooperation. It would be better if he let her know what was going on. "If they sabotaged an airplane, why wouldn't they pay a low-level government official a little money to keep people away from the wreck so they could get to it first?"

Comprehension dawned in her gaze, quickly followed by denial. "Do you have any evidence of that?"

"I've got a gut feeling about this, and I never ignore my sixth sense." His voice softened with each word.

Suddenly their physical closeness, his mouth mere inches from hers, roared through him. His hand rested by her left ear, and her long hair under his hand felt luxurious. Unconsciously, his fingers flexed. The heat he felt sparked in her eyes. His gaze focused on her mouth. Unable to stop himself, he brushed his lips over hers. They were softer than he expected, beckoning him to taste them further. He settled his mouth firmly over hers. She moaned and her lips parted. His tongue swept over her teeth and tasted the sweet nectar of her mouth.

A noise in the hall brought reality crashing back to him. He jerked away from her and stood. "Get dressed. We'll leave in five minutes."

"What about the medical supplies we were to bring?"

"Don't worry. I've got everything under control."

He stood and headed for the door. He didn't need this kind of torture. He went back to his room and gathered up his backpack and the beacon finder. By the time he'd collected everything and walked into the hall, Abigail was just opening the door to her room. She was dressed in a baggy shirt and long, loose slacks. Thick socks and heavy shoes graced her feet.

Elijah tried to hide his surprise that she was ready. She didn't say anything but closed the door.

"Lead the way," she said.

Abigail followed him down the corridor to the

stairs at the far end of the hallway. He said nothing, hoping that she wouldn't question why they were taking the stairs instead of the elevator. Luckily, she followed him without protest. At eleven o'clock at night, it should've been impossible to find a vacant taxi, but it wasn't. A taxi whizzed to a stop in front of them. After they stored their luggage in the trunk and were seated, Elijah turned to Abigail. "Tell him we want to go to the river docks."

After she related the instructions in Portuguese to the driver, she eyed Elijah. There were questions in her eyes, but she didn't voice them.

As they rode together in the taxi, Elijah made no move to fill her in on what they were doing. He wanted to test her. Would she follow him without question, or would the independent streak he sensed in her outweigh everything else? That knowledge might make the difference in a life-and-death situation further down the road.

Much to his surprise, she sat back and looked out the window. He felt her unspoken questions as clearly as if she'd voiced them. It was as if they were both tuned into the same invisible frequency. The awful thought occurred to him that if he could so easily read her, could she do the same with him?

It took less than five minutes to arrive at their destination. After Elijah paid the driver, he led Abigail to the dock. Halfway down it, a man appeared from one of the boats and greeted Elijah. He was an agent Elijah had recruited years ago to gather information on what was happening in Central America.

"Do you have everything I asked for?" Elijah asked his old friend.

"Yes."

Elijah glanced around the deserted dock. "What about a guide to take us upriver?"

"He's waiting for us on the boat."

Elijah nodded.

Abigail was irritated by Elijah's lack of manners, avoiding all introductions, then she realized that perhaps spies operated on their own code that had nothing to do with common politeness.

"Lead the way," Elijah told the other man. He glanced over his shoulder at Abigail. "You coming?"

"I made my choice in Kentucky," she snapped, irritated with this cloak-and-dagger stuff. "I haven't changed my mind."

Her answer must have amused him, because he smiled. And Abigail decided that smile was powerful enough to knock the socks off of any female under the age of ninety. Too bad the man didn't use it more often. Or maybe it was better he didn't. He probably could break the hearts of half the population of Virginia where he lived.

They followed the man along the dock to where it turned, and he stopped by a boat halfway down the long run. Another man rose from the boat and climbed onto the dock. The agent introduced them. The Indian's name was unpronounceable to Elijah.

"Does he speak English?" Elijah asked.

The agent shook his head. "He speaks Portuguese and his own native tongue."

Abigail spoke to the Indian in the native dialect she'd learned as a child. He shook his head, telling her in Portuguese that he didn't know that dialect. She explained this to Elijah.

Elijah shook the agent's hand. "Thanks for everything.'' He turned to Abigail. ''Tell our guide that I want to leave now.'' She translated.

The guide shook his head, then rattled off an answer.

''Our guide says it would be unwise to travel at night.''

Elijah nodded. ''I understand, but can he take us just beyond the city, and we could spend the balance of the night on the banks of the river?''

She related Elijah's request to the guide, who eyed Elijah.

''Tell him, Abigail, that if we wait until sunrise, there will be men here who will try to stop us. He will have to give back the money that my friend gave him.''

Elijah carefully watched the man as Abigail spoke to him. Elijah didn't like the calculating look that entered the other man's eyes, but the native nodded and spoke.

''You got your way, Elijah. He will take us to the edge of the city.''

Elijah's gaze met hers, and he let his satisfaction show.

As they were pulling away from the dock, she turned to Elijah. ''Are you always used to getting your way?'' she softly asked.

''Not always, but I give it my best shot.''

A smile curved her mouth. ''I think you always manage.''

His deep laugh floated around her. ''I wish I could claim all the success you credit me with. Unfortunately, in the real world, success isn't so easy. Sometimes, there are circumstances beyond my control.''

She arched her brow. "I bet you work hard to make those circumstances as few as possible."

He had the oddest feeling that she'd nailed him. But how? He hadn't said anything that would give away his thoughts.

Yet the impression that she understood him persisted. No one over the last few years had come so close to the bone as Abigail just had. He was known among his colleagues as an enigma. His boss, Neil, complained that Elijah was the perfect spy—a man with no feelings that could betray him. Yet here was this woman—a stranger who hadn't met him until yesterday—able to peg his emotions and motives with seeming ease. It was uncanny. Spooky.

Her eyes continued to search his. She was wanting an answer, and he felt himself responding to her.

"That's my job, Abigail. To make sure odds are in my agents' favor, to lessen the chances that things will go wrong."

"And you're good at your job, aren't you, Elijah?" From the sure look in her eyes, her question was more of a statement. One that didn't require an answer. But answer he did.

"I try."

They fell silent as their guide took them beyond the city and found a spot on the bank were they could land. The guide beached the boat on the shallow bottom, then hopped out. Elijah joined him and helped pull it onto the bank.

Elijah held out his hands to Abigail. "Let me help you." His strong hands grasped her sides and lifted her out of the boat. The Indian handed blankets to Abigail and Elijah, then he took a third blanket, threw it over his shoulders and lay down on his side.

Abigail still hadn't caught up with her sleep, and tiredness pulled at her. Wrapping the blanket around her, she stretched out on the ground. Elijah lay down beside her.

"Are you all right?" he whispered.

Her eyes flew open to study him. "Yes, why wouldn't I be?"

The guide spoke to Abigail. She turned to Elijah. "He said that we'll leave at first light. The village where my parents lived is about a half-day's journey from here."

Elijah studied her intently. After a long silence, he asked, "Are you sure you're feeling all right? You haven't had much sleep lately."

"I'm fine."

"Okay," he said, then continued in a different vein. "I arrived about five-thirty yesterday morning, you weren't there. I was only going to give you a few more minutes before I called the sheriff to see if he could locate you."

She grinned. "I wish I could've seen you if you had confronted the sheriff. That would've been a sight to behold."

He pulled the blanket higher around his shoulders. "And why is that?"

"Sheriff Box is a force unto himself."

Her words intrigued him. "What do you mean?"

"The sheriff is rather laid-back. Nothing seems to ruffle his feathers—except when you Washington types try to push him." She leaned closer to him. "If you ever run across him, don't let his mountain manner fool you. He's got a mind like a steel trap. He enjoys toying with sophisticated law enforcement agents."

"You don't think he would've cooperated?"

"Yes, but in his own good time. I remember one time when an FBI agent came to the mountain and wanted Sheriff Box to rush out to a particular man's house on the mountain. The agent thought it was of national importance. Sheriff Box looked at the paperwork the agent had, then went to lunch before he showed the agent where Henry lived. Henry wasn't the man they wanted. The sheriff knew it and tweaked the agent's nose a bit. He would've loved you, Elijah."

The vision she called up in his head made Elijah grateful not to have met the man. After a pause, he said, "Go to sleep, Abigail. Dawn will come quickly."

He rolled up in his blanket, then tried to clear his mind, to find peaceful images that would relax him. The only images that came to mind were Abigail and her lips, which left his body aching and unsatisfied.

An hour later, Elijah closed his eyes again and listened to the sound of the jungle at night. The river rushed by, and the sound of scurrying animals punctuated the darkness. The wind rustled the leaves of the towering trees.

Things certainly weren't going as he'd planned them. Hell, from the instant he'd spotted Abigail getting out of her car, nothing seemed to have gone smoothly. The attraction he felt for her had blindsided him, leaving him scrambling to recover his composure. You're losing it, old boy, he told himself.

His actions were guided simply by the need to get to the plane first, no matter what it took. Too bad his heart didn't buy the argument, and too bad his body didn't act like it. The last thought that crossed his brain before he fell asleep was that he was in real trouble.

It was the smell that woke her. It was wrong. There was no tangy scent of pine and tart crispness to the air. Instead, a heaviness surrounded her. The quiet serenity of her mountain home was replaced by the sounds of birds crying out, leaves rustling and water flowing close by.

"It's time to get up, Abigail," Elijah's low voice whispered in her ear.

And that was wrong, too. The sound of a man's voice in her ear as she woke. She wondered what it would be like to wake with that voice every morning. She clamped down hard on the errant thought. She didn't need the extra grief of wishing for things that could never be, no matter how attracted she was to the man.

She turned toward him and met his gaze. His brown eyes seemed to penetrate straight to her heart, reading all her secret thoughts. She threw her arm over her eyes.

He chuckled. "Why do I get the feeling you're not a morning person?"

She eyed him. "It's not that. It's just…"

He waited.

She shook her head.

"There's coffee and bananas for breakfast."

She propped herself up on her elbows and glanced around the clearing. The guide stood by the boat, re-arranging the supplies.

She glanced at Elijah. He was studying her.

"Dare I ask how you're feeling this morning?"

She pushed a lock of her shoulder-length hair off

her face. "Like I'm a normal person, not a zombie from a horror flick."

He studied her, then nodded. "We need to get going."

She scrambled to her feet and started walking to the thick foliage behind them.

"Where are you going?"

She paused and, looking over her shoulder, gave him a pointed look. Her cheeks were red with embarrassment. "I need a moment alone."

"Oh." Being the smart man that he was, he immediately caught her unstated meaning. He turned his back to her and watched the river.

She finished quickly. After washing her hands in the river, she returned to the fire and picked up the tin cup on a rock and quickly downed the contents. The rich taste of the Brazilian coffee danced over her tongue and slid down her throat in a heavenly wave. She moaned her enjoyment. Suddenly, she had the feeling she was being watched. Her eyes popped open to find Elijah staring at her with an intensity that made her shake.

Her tongue seemed to swell, making it hard to talk. "It's delicious coffee. Unlike anything I can get in the States." She had the oddest feeling that although Elijah heard her, none of her words registered with him. He was in another world.

She needed to say something. Anything. "I got spoiled when we were down here—the fresh beans. Uh—there's no other taste like it in the world."

Suddenly, as if someone had snapped his fingers, Elijah came out of his trance. "You ready to go?" he asked.

She handed the tin cup to the guide and then turned to Elijah. "Yes."

"Good, because we can't afford to waste any more time."

She had the oddest feeling that he wasn't talking about their trip.

It was then she noticed the holster clipped to his belt. The gun inside didn't look small. "Are you expecting trouble?" She pointed to the gun.

"You tell me, Abigail. Is it wise to walk through the jungle without some form of protection?"

He had a point, but she didn't like it. "I don't think you'll need it."

"It's my sincere hope that I won't. But it would be foolish not to have a weapon. Rest assured, I know how to use it."

His reassurance didn't have the effect he wished.

It was early afternoon when the guide brought the boat to the shore and got out.

"What is he doing?" Elijah asked.

She inquired, then quietly listened to the answer. "The small tributary that you see ahead is the one that goes by the village where my parents lived."

"Why isn't he guiding the boat that way? Why are we stopping here?" Elijah inquired.

The guide's face reminded her of several stone totems that she had seen over the years. She asked him again why he was unloading the boat.

He stopped and stared at them, then answered.

Abigail's heart sank when she heard his answer.

"What did he say?" Elijah demanded.

"He says this is as far as he'll go. Years ago, men from the village where we are going killed his brother. He's scared to go there. Scared of the villagers.''

Elijah couldn't believe his ears. "The hell you say.''

She flinched. "I don't lie, Elijah.''

He glared at her. "If he won't take us there, why did he tell my man he would?''

She translated and waited patiently as the Indian answered.

"He said his family needs the money. According to him, the village is maybe an hour's walk from here. All we have to do is follow the river.''

Elijah's hand went to the gun at his waist. She laid her hand over his, stopping his movement. He glared at her.

"I don't think threatening to shoot him will make a difference. Look at his eyes. He is afraid.''

Elijah cursed, the harsh sound causing her and the guide to wince.

"Please, Elijah, don't force the issue. The village is not very far from here. The terrain is familiar to me now.''

"I don't have the time to mess with his hang-ups.''

Abigail didn't wait for Elijah, but stepped out of the boat into the shallow water. She picked up the bag that had the first aid supplies in it.

"What are you doing?'' he asked harshly.

"I'm walking to the village.''

She heard him curse under his breath, then scramble out of the boat. He threw their supplies on the ground and turned to Abigail. "You tell this miserable coward that these supplies better be here when I send someone back for them or I'll make sure he visits this village and gets what's coming to him.''

She hesitated.

"Tell him, dammit. Word for word." Fire blazed from Elijah's eyes.

She did. The man looked relieved, then nodded his head. They watched him hop into the boat and continue upstream.

When Elijah looked at her, his eyes were still fierce with anger. She would well imagine how he could intimidate an enemy.

"We'll send villagers back for the supplies." Her words didn't seem to comfort him.

"What if someone steals them?"

"Elijah, there isn't a lot of traffic up and down this tributary. If any of the tribesmen come across them, they'll leave them. There's really nothing to worry about."

She shrugged and started toward the village, praying that they would find a warm welcome. She didn't think Elijah would appreciate any more changes in his plan, and if there were changes, she didn't want to be around to see his reaction.

Chapter 4

In spite of Elijah's foul temper, a quiet peacefulness settled over Abigail as she moved through the jungle. She was going home to a well-beloved place; the smell, the humidity, the vibrant colors were familiar and calming. She could almost hear her father instruct her on how to survive in this place.

A pain shot through her heart at the thought of her father. She closed her eyes and swallowed the lump in her throat. Why did he have to die?

She heard Elijah curse, followed by the sound of skin slapping skin. Turning, she saw him holding his neck.

"What happened?" she asked, imagining all sorts of different tragedies.

"They've got mosquitoes the size of a 747," he sourly informed her.

The humor of the moment overwhelmed her and

she laughed. "And don't forgot the ticks and black-flies in the right season."

He scowled, giving her a look she was sure made many a man quake in his boots. "Thanks for the encouragement."

She tried to swallow her mirth, but didn't succeed. This handsome, very masculine, intense man got bitten by mosquitoes like a normal person. Perhaps the little bugs didn't realize what a high-powered man he was. The impudent thought made her want to giggle, but she resisted the temptation, thinking that Elijah wouldn't find any amusement in the situation. "Didn't you put on mosquito repellent before we left the city?"

His expression was sour. "Obviously not."

"Perhaps the bugs don't know who you are?" The instant the words were out of her mouth, she wanted to call them back. But her comment didn't annoy him as she expected. Instead, a deep chuckle rumbled up from his chest.

"Touché, Ms. McGee." He studied her. "Why aren't the mosquitoes bothering you?"

She shrugged, then slipped off her backpack and unzipped the pouch, looking for the mosquito repellent she'd put in there this morning. "It's probably the garlic pills I take. My blood isn't as tasty as yours."

He arched his brow. "I doubt that."

She ignored his dubious compliment. "Besides, I put on some repellent this morning when I went off into the jungle. You should've done the same instead of getting out your gun. You could shoot them, but I think this will be more effective." She grabbed the tube and handed it to him.

He frowned as he took the repellent from her and began to smear the ointment on his exposed skin. "You remember all this scenery?" he asked as he screwed the cap back onto the tube.

Her gaze traveled around the area, taking in the tall trees that reached to the heavens for light while offering shade to the animals below. At each level of the jungle a unique ecosystem existed. She could recite each system in her sleep since her mother had made sure that her children knew as much as possible about the place where they lived. Not only did they learn about the local plants, they received a college-level biology class.

"Oh, yes. My mother was very firm that we learn about where we lived. Did you know the Amazon and its eleven hundred tributaries carry one fifth of all the fresh water in the world? It dumps about ten billion liters per second of fresh water into the Atlantic, pushing back the salty seawater for one hundred and sixty miles offshore. And you see how the jungle is divided into five distinct layers—"

He laid his hand on her arm, startling her out of her well-remembered speech.

"I really don't want a biology lesson, Abigail. All I want to do is retrieve what we came for and get the h—" he cleared his throat "—heck out of here."

He handed the ointment back to her. His fingers brushed hers, making little sparks of electricity race up her arm. She ignored the feeling and replaced the ointment in the pack, then slipped it on her back. "Mother made sure that we weren't lacking in our studies. As a matter of fact, when we went back to the States, my sister, Leah, and I were almost two years ahead of our schoolmates, and in biology we smoked them all.'' There was a touch of pride in her voice.

With painful clarity, she remembered having to sit in class with the seniors, who were all seventeen, and she barely fifteen. She hadn't been friends with any of them. When she finally shook off the bitter memories, she found herself pinned by Elijah's keen stare. She had the awful feeling that he had read everything that had been in her heart, and she had no desire to share those painful memories with this stranger.

''So you ended up in classes where you were the youngest and out of place.''

His observation was right on the mark, nearly taking her breath away. And since he'd understood her feelings, there was no need to say anything further. She resumed walking, but wondered what experience he'd lived through that gave him that insight.

''Be sure to keep your eye out for alligators. They like to sun themselves on the riverbank.'' She threw the warning over her shoulder.

He looked around. ''Anything else I need to keep my eyes peeled for?''

She thought a minute. ''Let's see. Jaguars and anacondas. But unless you're in the river, the anacondas shouldn't be a problem. They're not a poisonous snake. They squeeze their victims to death.''

''Is that all?''

She thought for a moment. The capybaras, which were the world's largest rodents, wouldn't prove a problem. Nor would the porcupines or vampire bats that they might see. ''Nothing I can think of.''

He fell into step beside her. After a few minutes, he wiped the sweat off his forehead and asked, ''Is it always this humid down here?''

The air was like a thick, wet blanket, making a person fight for breath. She glanced at him, her eyebrows arched. "This is the dry season, Elijah. A walk in the park, so to speak. The rainy season isn't for another three months."

"Well, hell." He shook his head. "And I thought hell was hot and dry. My mistake." After he wiped the moisture from his forehead and took a calming breath, he asked, "What do you think our reception will be once we reach the village?"

That same question had nagged at Abigail all morning, slipping up on her when she was least expecting it. She didn't have a clue as to what their reception would be. Her parents had been loved by the villagers, and she and her sister held in great esteem. But that had been years ago, before the current troubles of the vanishing jungle and rape of the land. "I don't know. I wish I did, but I don't."

The missionary organization to which her parents had belonged normally kept in contact with the missionaries, telling them how the work was progressing in the region they had worked. But Abigail had made it clear to them that she didn't want to know anything about the jungle. Too bad her adverse attitude was coming back to bite her now. Her parents would've been appalled by her reaction, but they weren't around to advise her. Of course, she wasn't going to tell Elijah that. It was bad enough that she was tromping through the growth with him. She didn't have to bare her soul to him, too.

Besides, even if she had kept in touch, the forces in Brazil had changed drastically over the last fifteen years. Much of the rain forest had been clear-cut to make ranches and farms. The only problem with that was the soil was so poor that most of the farms failed. Even the ranches struggled to produce enough feed for the cattle. She didn't know how this particular tribe had fared or what their feelings toward outsiders were now. They had been wary of strangers years ago. Now she couldn't even begin to guess at their feelings.

"I hope you're good at ad-libbing, Elijah, because I think we're going to need it."

A light twinkled in his eyes. "That's what I do best, Abigail."

"I hope so, because I have the strange feeling that I'm going to witness your skill firsthand." And she wasn't too happy about it.

"They left sometime during the night," Lorenzo Villa said into the telephone.

"So they slipped out without you knowing about it?" the man at the other end of the line said.

Lorenzo didn't like what the man was implying. That this mess was his fault. "Yes, Elijah is very clever. He also brought with him a woman who was raised among the tribe where the plane has gone down."

"Abigail McGee," he said before Lorenzo could name her.

"You know of this woman?" Lorenzo sounded surprised.

"Yes, her parents worked as teachers and translators among the tribe. They were the first white people the Indians allowed in their village. When is the group you're taking to the site going to be ready?"

"As soon as I finish talking to you, we're going to leave."

"Hurry. Elijah can't be trusted."

When he hung up, the man ran his fingers through his hair. If Elijah got to that information first, it would be over for him. That is, unless he could discredit Elijah.

And he would try his best to do that.

The skies opened up and the deluge soaked both Abigail and Elijah before they could take cover under a large tree.

"I thought you said this was the dry season?" Elijah complained.

"That's right. So if this is an example of how it rains during the dry season, imagine what it's like during the rainy season."

It was a thought he could do without.

They sat at the base of the tree and looked out into the rain.

"This sure puts a crimp in our plan to get to the village," he grumbled. "Our head start is down the toilet."

She glanced at him. "Don't worry, Elijah. It's probably raining like this in Boa Vista. No one will start off in this."

He wished he could take comfort in her reassurance.

After about a half hour, the rain stopped as if someone had turned off a faucet.

Abigail stood. "Let's get going."

He followed.

As they walked through the dripping jungle, Elijah sensed Abigail's mixed feelings about this place. Although it was more than obvious she knew what she was doing, walking close to the stream, keeping an eye out for any poisonous snakes and alligators, keeping a walking stick by her side to probe the ground before them, he read in her eyes a certain disquiet. What ghosts was she battling?

He shook his head. Why did he care what was bothering her? He was here to simply retrieve the courier's pouch and discover who the mole was in the upper echelons of the CIA, not mess around in Abigail's life.

Yet, in spite of his attempts to tell himself it was none of his business what was going on in her head, he couldn't help but be concerned. If it wasn't for him, she wouldn't be here right now, reliving old nightmares, seeing old dreams. He knew he certainly wouldn't want to go back to Oklahoma and revisit some of the foster homes where he'd lived. That part of his life was best forgotten. That's why he felt so crummy about putting Abigail in this situation. He felt downright guilty, but there had been no choice. Catching that mole outweighed any guilt he was experiencing. But that didn't mean he couldn't be concerned.

He lightly grasped her arm, bringing her to a halt. Her questioning gaze met his.

"Are you all right, Abigail?"

Surprise flitted across her face. For an instant, he thought she was going to level with him, but instead, her emotions seemed to close down.

"Of course."

He continued to study her. She turned away from him and began to walk.

As he followed behind her, Elijah felt like slime for putting her through this.

* * *

It was late afternoon when they were suddenly surrounded by Indians from the village to which they were heading. The crowd of dark-skinned men seemed to have magically dropped from the sky. They were dressed in loose-fitting shirts and long pieces of cloth that were wrapped around their waists and came down to their knees. The natives called the cloth *wannat,* and it was like an Indonesia sarong.

Elijah tensed, his hand going toward the gun on his belt. Abigail held out her hand, stopping him. "These are the very people you want to help us. It wouldn't be wise to draw your gun against them," she softly told him.

Elijah glanced at her, then at the men. He slowly lowered his arms. The Indians responded by easing their stances.

Abigail gave the men the traditional greeting of the village. Although she had rarely spoken the Indian dialect in the last fifteen years, it came back quickly. There was surprise in the Indians' eyes when she murmured the words. She next introduced herself and Elijah to them and explained that they were heading toward the village.

One of the men stepped forward. "How can you prove you are who you say you are?" he asked in his own dialect.

The question caught Abigail by surprise.

Stepping close, Elijah asked, "What's wrong?"

"They want proof of who I am."

"Show them your driver's license," Elijah answered.

"I could, but they probably don't read English." She rubbed her chin, then a light entered her eyes. "I could tell them a story of my time in the village."

Elijah frowned.

Abigail turned to the gathered men. "On my tenth birthday, I decided I was old enough to climb one of the trees around the village and get myself a monkey that I had been begging my mother to get me. I fell and broke my arm. The arm didn't mend right, and I was taken to Caracas for an operation." She unbuttoned her sleeve and rolled it up to her elbow to show the Indians the scar. "Not only did I fall that day, but Rani, my friend, was with me. She also fell and broke her arm."

One of the Indians stepped forward. "I remember this. My sister was greatly punished by our parents."

"Den?" Abigail vividly remembered Rani's older brother. She and Rani had followed him around, giving him no end of grief.

The Indian nodded.

"It is good to see you, old friend. Rani and I pestered you when we were children."

"You speak the truth." He offered his hand in friendship.

Several of the men smiled and began to talk among themselves.

"What are they saying?" Elijah whispered.

"They're glad an old friend has come back."

Several of the Indians stepped forward, introduced themselves and shook her hand, sharing memories of her childhood. Abigail grinned, glad Elijah couldn't understand the dialect so her childish exploits were still unknown to him. She wasn't too sure she wanted to be reminded of the incidents, either.

As the men prepared to return to the village, Abigail explained that their supplies had been left several miles back where the smaller branch of the river

joined the main body. Three of the men turned, re-
tracing their steps to retrieve their supplies. The others
accompanied Elijah and Abigail to the village.

When they started walking to the village again, Elijah fell into step beside her.

"What did they say?" he asked.

As much as she hoped he wouldn't ask, Abigail
didn't think Elijah would let this incident slip.

"Each man introduced himself, then recalled a
treasured memory he had of me or my parents. It is
a wonderful custom among the tribe members."

"Is that why you were looking a little green there
when that second Indian related his story?"

Her startled gaze flew to his.

A self-satisfied expression settled on his face.
"You want to tell me what he said?"

Determination hardened her jaw. "No."

"You came as a translator. You're not doing your
job."

"Oh, I plan to do my job. But what the Indians
shared has nothing to do with your plane."

Surprise colored his eyes, then he laughed. "Boy,
those memories must've been whoppers."

She frowned.

After several minutes, Elijah whispered, "Do you
think they will help?"

"It's hard to say. A lot has happened here in the
last few years. As you already know, this tribe wasn't
too friendly to outsiders in the first place. Now...who
can say?"

"But you're not an outsider. That's why I sought
you out," Elijah pointed out.

"You've got a point, Elijah. But things don't stay

the same. At one time I was considered part of the tribe, but—'' She shrugged.

His jaw hardened.

''I wish I could tell you they are taking us to the village to welcome us. But I can't. Obviously, they remember my parents—''

''And you.''

She threw him a dark look. ''And me. I pray they'll greet us warmly. That's all I can do.''

''Terrific,'' she heard him grumble.

As they entered the outskirts of the village, people stopped their activities and stared at them. Although there wasn't open hostility in their gazes, there was a wariness that set Abigail's nerves on edge.

The village was exactly the way Abigail remembered it. Conical huts spiraled out from the center area where the communal cooking and work was conducted. Several women were working on the evening meal. On the outer edge of the village, just as they entered, was a large patch of ground where the Indians farmed vegetables. On the river side of the village, Abigail could see the day's catch hanging on the drying poles the Indians had rigged.

As they made their way through the village, they collected more and more people, who pointed and whispered until they stopped at a hut near the center of the village.

''Samuel,'' one of the Indians called out. ''We have visitors you will want to see,'' he said in his native tongue.

Abigail understood perfectly what the Indian had said and prepared herself to see the man who had been her parents' helper while they lived here. Samuel had had a passion to learn, to know the world outside his village. Her parents had opened up that world for him.

After a moment, a man emerged from the hut. He was taller than the average Indian, with powerful arms and a deep chest. Although his hair was completely gray, there were no age lines on his face. When he turned and looked at her, Abigail saw the color of his eyes. They were light gray, a legacy from his explorer father, and she remembered looking into those kind eyes when she was growing up.

She took a step toward the man. "Samuel."

"Abigail?" He turned his head slightly, not quite able to believe it was her. "Abigail McGee."

She nodded, tears welling in her eyes. She had no idea that Samuel was back in the village. He took a step toward her and swept her into a big bear hug and whirled her around.

"Ah, it is so good to see you, child," he said in his native dialect, setting her back down. "You have grown up since I last saw you."

She grinned. "It's been nearly ten years."

"Has it been that long?" he asked, shaking his head. "I was sorry to hear about your parents. They hold a special place in my heart."

She choked back her tears. "Thank you, Samuel."

Elijah stepped close to Abigail. "What's he saying?" He nodded toward Samuel.

"He was greeting me," she explained.

"You know this man?" Elijah asked.

She wiped her cheeks. "Yes. Elijah Kendrick, this is Samuel Sotit." She made the introduction in English, since Samuel had learned English from her parents. "He was my parents' student while we lived in this village."

The men shook hands.

"Things have changed since that time," Samuel explained. "After I went to college, I became a minister and am now the pastor of the church in this village."

Her eyes went round, and an odd feeling spread through her chest. A smile, a reflection of her joy, broke across her mouth.

"Why are you here at this time, Abigail?" Samuel asked.

"We need help from you and the villagers, Samuel," Abigail explained.

The tall Indian studied both Abigail and Elijah.

"Come inside and we will talk. Later, we will meet with the other villagers so that you may greet them."

Abigail nodded and followed Samuel inside his hut. He quickly made the introductions of his wife and two daughters.

"Sometimes, I look at those faces and think of you and your sister," Samuel said to Abigail. "I liked to tease your father about only having girls. Perhaps I've been taught a lesson. But—" he held up his hand "—I would not trade my daughters for anything."

Maya, his wife, arched her brow. "That is why I am expecting again," she said in English. "We wish for another girl."

The look on Samuel's face was priceless. Abigail tried with all her might to avoid showing any emotion at Maya's comment, but a tiny smile slipped out.

The main room of the hut was without furniture, and Elijah looked around for a place to sit. Samuel and his wife sat on the floor. Abigail joined them, sitting cross-legged. They all looked up at Elijah.

"Are you going to sit?" Abigail softly asked.

He quickly sat beside Abigail.

"Now, tell me what it is you need help with," Samuel said in English.

Elijah opened his mouth, but Abigail touched his hand and met his gaze with hers. She silently warned him that he needed to follow her lead. A muscle in Elijah's jaw jumped, but she immediately understood that he would comply. A spark of admiration flared in her heart. Elijah was sticking to his part of their bargain. He was letting her take the lead.

Since both Samuel and Maya had spoken English, Abigail decided to relay the reason for their visit in English so Elijah could follow what was said. "Two nights ago, an airplane went down in the jungle close by. Elijah came to me and explained about the plane. He is hoping that some of the villagers will help us to locate the plane's position.

"The plane was one that our government was using to carry important information. Also, one of Elijah's friends was aboard. He longs to know if the ten passengers survived the crash." Abigail prayed that Elijah was a good actor and would follow her lead, but if the past twelve hours were any indication, he would be more than up to the job.

"I see." Samuel's tone was not encouraging.

Elijah leaned forward. "Have you seen the plane?"

"No." Samuel shook his head. "But—"

"But what?" Elijah asked impatiently. Abigail gently touched his forearm. When he met her gaze, she tried silently to school him in patience. He must have correctly read her message, because his body seemed to relax.

"Two nights ago, I woke and I thought I had heard something." Samuel shrugged. "Some of our men set out the next morning to look, but have not yet returned.''

"I was hoping you might speak to the villagers about helping us search for this plane," Abigail explained.

"No."

Samuel's answer was such a shock, Abigail simply stared at him.

"Explain to her, husband," Maya urged Samuel. "Your answer seems very harsh to her."

Samuel sighed. "Two years ago a man from the government came to the village and asked for my help. There was a road that needed to be built. They cut down much more of our jungle than they had promised. Several of our young men worked on the road, caught yellow fever and died. I had to bury them and then face their parents. I made a vow to never again speak for an outside force that wanted my people's help. I am here to protect them."

"But I wouldn't ask them to do—"

Samuel held up his hand. "I cannot."

Abigail's mind raced. "Would you object if I asked for their help?"

"No, but there might be a problem."

Elijah became very still, and Abigail felt his gaze on her.

Ignoring Elijah, she asked Samuel, "What's that?"

"I'm surprised that you don't remember the village customs and protocol."

Elijah tensed.

Her gaze didn't waver from Samuel. "Please tell me what I am forgetting."

"Are you married to this—" Samuel pointed to Elijah "—man?"

Her eyes went wide. "N-no," she stammered.

"You are still single, no?" Samuel continued.

Memories of the customs of the tribe came flooding back to Abigail. A sick feeling settled in the pit of her stomach. "Yes, I'm single."

"Then the villagers will not allow you to speak at the festivities tonight," Samuel said.

A deep sigh escaped Abigail's lips.

"What's going on?" Elijah demanded.

Samuel turned to Elijah. "The villagers will not listen to an unmarried woman. It is not done. Unmarried women are never allowed to speak to the village on issues. If Abigail was married, her status would be determined by her husband. Even if she was married to you, the villagers would listen because she was the daughter of old friends."

In the urgency of the moment, when Elijah showed up on her doorstep, Abigail hadn't thought about how she'd be greeted and about the customs of the people. She remembered how the tribe had acted so circumspectly around her mother, her and her sister. They were treated with the respect and dignity that her father's position as a man of learning afforded them.

Elijah stared at Abigail. "Why didn't you mention this earlier?"

"If you'll recall, you showed up rather suddenly and didn't give me any time to think."

Abigail stood and walked to the window in the hut, looking out at the center point of the village where the evening dinner was being prepared. She felt Elijah's presence behind her.

"So you're telling me that in order for you to ask for help you have to be married?" he asked.

Abigail couldn't quite look at him. "Yes." She

was so embarrassed that she wished the earth would open and swallow her up. "I didn't think about this custom because I thought Samuel would speak for us."

"Couldn't he interpret my request?" Elijah asked.

"No," Samuel answered. "I will not lend my hand to this."

After a moment of silence, Elijah looked at Abigail. "All right, we'll just pretend to be married."

Both Samuel and Abigail stared at him as if he'd grown another head.

"What's the problem?" Elijah asked, truly puzzled by their response.

Samuel crossed his arms over his chest. "I cannot lie to my people."

"What?" Elijah yelped.

Abigail's gaze slipped from Elijah's fiery one. "I can't ask Samuel to lie, Elijah. He's the pastor of these people. What kind of example would he be if he lied?"

Elijah's glare didn't lessen.

"Everyone lies," Elijah spat back.

Shaking her head, she whispered, "You're wrong. I understand in your business that you'd find our attitude odd, but…" She shrugged. "Next time, don't take the daughter of missionaries on one of your missions."

Elijah looked as if she'd just hit him with a wide plank. Then his eyes narrowed. "All right. We'll get married."

Now Abigail was the one who felt off-center and unbalanced.

"Well?" Elijah turned to Samuel. "Why not marry

us now, then tonight Abigail can address the villagers.''

Abigail continued to stare at Elijah, unable to believe her ears.

"Will that satisfy everyone?" Elijah asked.

It was a clever way to get around everyone's objections, she admitted to herself. It was becoming increasingly obvious to Abigail that Elijah let nothing get in the way of doing a job. As much as she wanted to, she couldn't find an objection to his plan. She had agreed to help him. Later, when they went back to the States, she could file for an annulment.

"Yes," Samuel answered with an accompanying nod.

Abigail noticed that Elijah didn't ask her if she objected. "Has anyone ever told you that you're too clever for your own good?"

"Nope." He stepped to her side and folded her hand in his. "We're ready," he told Samuel, motioning for him to proceed.

Samuel eyed them both, then asked Abigail, "Do you want this?"

Her first inclination was to yell no. But if she didn't go along with him, what chance did anyone on the plane have? She had decided in Kentucky that she would do this, and she would see it to the end. "Yes."

Samuel nodded. His wife went outside and gathered several lianas blooming on one of the trees and brought them inside. She wove the vine on which the flowers grew into a circlet and put it on Abigail's head.

Elijah stood beside Abigail. They were dressed in their damp, wrinkled clothes, a far cry from the clothes she imagined she'd have on when she wed. He made no move to hold her hand, but stood stiffly by her side.

Samuel began to read from his prayer book. When he got to the part where they vowed their love through good and bad, she noticed an odd light in Elijah's eyes. When he repeated his vows, he didn't look away. His burning gaze kept hers captive, making her wonder what was going on in his head. When she said her vows, Elijah's gaze darkened.

"You may kiss your bride," Samuel ended.

Elijah turned to Abigail and slid his arms around her and his lips came down on hers. She didn't quite know what to expect, but it wasn't this warm, stomach-fluttering feeling that invaded her body. Samuel cleared his throat, hinting to Elijah to end the kiss.

Abigail felt the heat in her cheeks as embarrassment flooded her. Briefly, she glanced at Samuel and saw his satisfied grin. When she looked at Elijah, there was a glitter in his eyes that made her knees weak and her heart race.

Samuel motioned them toward the door. "We will have to go into the church for me to get the right documents to file. The government is very strict about such things. I will file them for you."

"Don't worry, Abigail," Elijah whispered in her ear. "When we get home, I won't expect you to be the loving wife." He bent his head so his mouth was beside her ear. "I'll file for divorce."

Her eyes met his. What could she say? Thanks? She looked away and wondered why she felt like she'd fallen down the rabbit hole and didn't know which way was up.

Samuel finished his part of the form, then presented

it to them to sign. After they did, Samuel beamed.
"Heaven works in ways that we don't always understand."

Abigail nodded and glanced at Elijah. Somehow,
she didn't believe he was an answer to her prayers.

Chapter 5

Samuel led them through the village, occasionally stopping to introduce old friends to Abigail. On the third introduction, Abigail recognized the young woman who held a toddler in her arms and had a small one clutching her leg.

"Rani? Is that you?" Abigail whispered in the native dialect.

The young woman smiled and nodded her head. Abigail stepped close and hugged the other woman.

"Look at you. A mother. I remember running through the jungle with you to avoid our mothers and the spankings we were going to get."

Rani grinned. "I view those spankings in a new light now that I am a mother."

"Where is your husband?" Abigail asked.

"You will see him tonight at the festivities."

Abigail felt a hand on her arm and looked up into

Elijah's questioning face. "Aren't you going to introduce me to your friend?"

The motivation for his request bothered Abigail. She didn't for one moment believe it came from politeness. Quickly, she made the introductions in English, which Rani knew, but when she reached the word *husband,* the word seemed to lodge in her throat.

"I'm Abigail's husband," Elijah smoothly supplied, his voice filled with charm and warmth. "So you knew Abigail when she was small and did things that made her parents crazy?"

Rani carefully studied Elijah. "Yes. But her secrets will be safe with me." She turned to Abigail. "I will see you tonight."

Elijah leaned close and whispered, "That's a lady I could use in the agency. One who knows when to talk and when to keep secrets."

"Don't even think about it," Abigail shot back.

When they reached the guest hut, Samuel pointed to the door. "I will leave you here. Your things are inside. Rest, and I will send food and drink for you." Samuel grasped Abigail's hand. "I am very glad to see you again. I am sorry it is sadness that brings you to us."

Her eyes teared, and a lump the size of a grapefruit seemed to lodge in her throat. Abigail tried to smile, but her emotions overwhelmed her. Instead, she threw her arms around Samuel and hugged him. "I'm so glad to see you."

Samuel pulled back, nodded at Elijah and walked away.

Unable to meet Elijah's knowing gaze, she turned and walked into the hut. Similar to Samuel's, it had one room, with woven mats on the floor and open windows that allowed a breeze to blow through.

Abigail went to the window and looked out at the village, trying to sort through the confused tangle of emotions bouncing through her head. Suddenly, she was married and seeing old friends that she never thought to see again. And then there were the memories of her parents. She had always hoped they would be with her on her special day. How ironic that she was in the very place where they had spent so much time and effort. She couldn't have chosen a better place to be married than here.

Too bad she didn't know or love the groom.

"I know that wasn't the kind of wedding you always hoped for," Elijah said quietly as he came to a stop beside her.

His words startled her, and her gaze flew to his. She read the pain of her loss in his eyes. It brought another lump to her throat. "No, it wasn't exactly what I'd planned on." A tear slipped from her eye.

His thumb gently brushed the moisture away. "For killing that dream, I'm sorry."

He could've said a thousand other things that wouldn't have gone straight to her heart like this did. But apparently Elijah had that gift of seeing a situation and knowing exactly the right thing to say. Suddenly her tears began in earnest. She tried to turn away from him, but he wouldn't let her. Instead, he wrapped his arms around her, resting his chin on her head.

"Go ahead, Abigail. Cry. It will help."

"How do you kn-ow?" she hiccupped.

"Trust me, I know," he whispered into her hair.

It was the earnestness of his voice that burst the

dam of her feelings, and tears came crashing through. The sharp pain from her parents' deaths reared its ugly head, and she again felt the loss.

After what seemed an eternity, her sobs trailed off. The first thing she noticed was the warmth and strength of Elijah's embrace.

His hand came up, cupped her chin so he could look in her eyes. "Are you feeling any better?"

"I'm feeling darn foolish right now," she answered, wiping the last of the moisture from her face.

His smile was incredibly gentle. "No, not foolish, Abigail. Gentle...sensitive...kind...but not foolish."

There was a knock on the door. Elijah answered it and took the tray of food and drink from the young Indian.

"Are you hungry or maybe thirsty?"

"I'd like something to drink." She gave him a small smile. "I've just lost a lot of moisture."

He looked around the empty room for a place to set the tray. Abigail took it from him and placed it on the floor, then sat cross-legged. She patted the floor beside her. He joined her.

She poured two glassfuls of the local drink, made from the fruit of the surrounding trees, that the Indians preferred, and handed him a glass. He tasted it, then smiled. "It's good." He took a banana from the tray. "Why did you do it?" he asked as he peeled the banana.

His question startled her and she looked at him. "Do what?"

His gaze bored into hers, and Abigail knew he was trying to read her emotions, trying to discern her motivations. "Agree to marry me."

Abigail knew at that instant never to try to play

cards with this man. He would probably remember every card that had been played and know every option that was left. Her dad had been like that. You could never slip anything by him. "What is there to say? We have to get to that crash site, and there was no other way for you and me to address the Indians. It had to be done."

He studied her for several minutes. "I know you're upset with how things turned out."

It was not what she expected him to say. "Not upset, just..." It was still hard to comprehend that she was this man's wife. Oh, granted, they were not the traditional bridal couple, but she always pictured herself loving the man she married—or at least knowing him. "I blame myself for not thinking about how things were done here." She hoped she sounded normal, instead of like a woman whose life had suddenly veered out of control. "I should've, but I didn't." Her voice reflected her discouragement.

"Well, if you're worried about the marriage, don't be. Believe me, this is only temporary. I'm not the marrying kind, and I don't have any hidden motives except to get this mission completed. When we get back to the States we can have the whole thing annulled."

Everything he said was true, and she had even thought it herself. Yet, the words pierced her heart. This was the second time a man wanted to marry her because of who she knew and what she could do for him. The knowledge left a bitter taste in her mouth.

"Why don't you rest, Abigail? Our dinner performance will be here all too quickly."

Elijah closed his eyes and listened to the sound of the village around him. He could hear the river in the background as it rushed by. The branches and leaves woven between the bracing poles allowed a cooling wind to bathe the interior of the hut.

When Samuel had announced that Abigail couldn't talk to the villagers if she was single, marrying her seemed the only logical choice. Nothing personal, no feeling, just the means to the end.

But Elijah had never planned on marrying after seeing the fiasco that was his parents' marriage. That relationship had been destructive and painful, and he vowed the day his dad died, he'd never make the same mistake his father had. This marriage to Abigail was only a sham. Period.

He glanced at the woman lying beside him. Dark circles colored the skin beneath her eyes, testifying to the fact that she'd started this trip exhausted, and so far she'd had little opportunity for much rest.

He lightly brushed back a strand of her blond hair. It felt like a baby's, soft and fine. There was a sprinkling of freckles across the bridge of her pert nose. He had the urge to kiss each one.

You're losing it, Elijah, he told himself, jerking his hand back. His actions today had been guided by the need to get to the plane, no matter what it took. He didn't even want to think about the other team following them.

But he chose to ignore the niggling doubt eating at him that his agreeing to marry Abigail simply because it was necessary wasn't quite true.

Lorenzo cursed as he watched the rain beat down in sheets. The unexpected storm had delayed their departure from the city, and how far they could go today depended on when the storm ended. He hoped the rain would let up within the next few minutes. If it did, they might make the village where the North Americans had gone before night. If not, then they wouldn't be able to make the entire journey today and would be forced to camp overnight, not getting to the village until tomorrow.

—

When she woke up, Abigail found herself curled into Elijah's embrace. Her head was tucked under his chin and her right hand rested on his chest. She should've been overheated this close to his big body. But oddly enough, she felt comfortable, as if this was where she should be. She lightly rubbed her palm over the well-developed chest. It was rock hard. She wondered what it felt like without his shirt on, her hand on his bare skin.

Realizing where her thoughts were taking her, she glanced up at Elijah's face to see if she could extract herself from this situation without him knowing about it. Unfortunately, when she glanced up, Elijah was calmly watching her.

"How long have you been awake?" she murmured, heat flooding her cheeks.

"Since the moment you opened your eyes."

Her heart plummeted. "Oh, sure. You felt my eyelashes open," she shot back, her embarrassment riding her hard.

It appeared he tried to swallow his grin. "No, it wasn't your eyelashes that woke me."

She stared at him a minute longer. "Well, are you going to tell me?"

"You're not going to like it."

Raising her eyebrow, she waited for him to answer.

"You wiggled that little butt of yours, which caused your thighs to brush against mine."

"Oh." She couldn't meet his gaze.

"I think there's something by the door you might want to look at," he softly told her.

Her head turned that direction to see what he was talking about. Inside the door, resting on their luggage and supplies, were clothes for the evening. She scrambled to her feet and picked up the wraps.

"I take it that's what we're to wear to the dinner tonight?" Elijah said as he sat up.

Abigail stared at the two pieces of cloth. She'd worn the traditional dress of the Indians when she was a child and had loved every minute of it. Somehow it didn't seem as exciting now as it had when she was ten, especially getting dressed in front of Elijah.

"Abigail, you all right?" he asked, coming to stand beside her.

Her head came up. "Yes. I was just thinking..."

"What?"

"We're going to have to get dressed in here."

He glanced around the room. "Yeah. What's the problem?"

Her jaw hardened and she glared at him. Was he being obtuse on purpose? Yes, he had to be. She knew from experience that Elijah knew exactly what he was doing. "That's the problem. I usually don't dress in front of strangers."

"But I'm your husband."

"Oh, please. Don't pull that excuse on me. If we hadn't had to get married to finish this mission, we'd still be strangers who knew little or nothing of each other."

He grasped her arm. "Don't worry about it, Abigail. I trust you won't peek."

Her jaw went slack in surprise. She walked over to the window opening and gazed out. Well, what a fine fix she found herself in. They had to change for the dinner tonight; tribal custom demanded it. They couldn't insult these people or they'd get nothing done. But the idea of changing in front of Elijah set her off her stride. The last person she'd shared a room with was her sister, years ago. This in no way compared to that situation.

"Abigail…" Rani's voice called from outside the hut. "Are you ready?"

Abigail raced over to the door and opened it.

Rani clicked her tongue in a gentle reprimand. "You must hurry and get ready. It is almost time for the banquet."

"We fell asleep," Abigail explained, feeling self-conscious and chagrined.

Rani glanced over Abigail's shoulder to Elijah. A small smile curved the Indian woman's mouth. "Do you wish for me to send my husband to yours to show him how to use the wrap to dress?"

An answer to a prayer, Abigail thought hastily. "Yes, please."

Rani nodded and disappeared around the side of the hut.

"She just pulled your butt out of the fire." Elijah's mouth was so close to her ear that she felt each of his words. His eyes danced with mirth. It was an expression that probably not many of his associates ever saw.

She handed him the wrap. "Here." She pushed him out the door. "Why don't you wait for Rani's husband outside?'' Before he could reply, she closed the door in his face, resting her forehead on the frame. She'd escaped this time. She just wondered how long she'd be so lucky.

A few minutes later, Abigail glanced down at the piece of cloth she'd wrapped around her in a sarong style. It was a modest dress, covering her from armpits to knees. But the thought of Elijah seeing her dressed like this threw her off balance.

''Get a grip,'' she scolded herself. If she wore shorts and a sleeveless shirt, she'd be showing more skin. Somehow her argument wasn't comforting.

Someone knocked on the hut door. ''Abigail?'' Rani called. ''Are you ready?''

Immediately Abigail opened the door. Rani was wearing a red dress and, behind her ear, an orchid.

''I brought you an orchid to wear this evening at the banquet.'' She held up the purple flower she had in her hand. ''Sit,'' Rani commanded, ''I will dress your hair.''

Abigail fingered the rubber band at the base of her neck. When she'd awakened this morning, her goal had been to keep her long hair tamed.

''Abigail, do you have a comb?'' Rani asked.

''Yes.'' Abigail retrieved it from her backpack and gave it to her friend.

A smile crept across Abigail's face. ''As I recall, you were good at fixing hair. Do you remember the time we tried to braid those passion flowers into our hair?''

Rani laughed. ''And we had monkeys coming out of the jungle all night to snatch the blossoms from our hair.''

''As I recall, the chief didn't think it was funny

when one of those animals messed on him." Abigail sat down in front of Rani.

Rani grimaced. "Don't remind me. My mother was so displeased that I was the one assigned to gather firewood for the next month."

"I remember. I had to do laundry for several weeks without help." Abigail felt Rani's fingers working out the strands of her hair. "How have things been here, my friend?"

Rani's hands stilled. "Not good. Many people have come through the jungle, looking for things. Gold, land, birds and monkeys." After a long pause, Rani asked, "Why have you returned, Abigail?"

"An American plane went down in the jungle somewhere around here."

"Oh."

"Elijah—"

"Your husband," Rani supplied.

"He knows one of the men on that plane. The man carried some important documents that Elijah needs." She glanced over her shoulder to Rani. "According to Elijah, he is not the only one who will be looking for the airplane. Others will no doubt come."

"You are sure of this?"

"Unfortunately, yes."

"Then you must warn the men so they will be aware others will come."

It hadn't occurred to Abigail to warn the Indians, but Rani was right. They needed to be prepared if others showed up. She nodded.

"How have you been?" Rani asked. "It has been many years since I saw you. You didn't keep in contact with us."

The simple reprimand pierced Abigail's heart. "My

parents died in a plane crash a couple of years after we left.''

''I know.'' Her friend's fingers stilled in Abigail's hair, as if waiting for further explanation.

Finally, Abigail admitted, ''I was mad and hurt, and I didn't want anything to remind me of them.''

Rani handed the comb back to Abigail, then placed the orchid behind Abigail's ear. When Abigail looked into her friend's eyes, there was a gentleness there. ''I wish you peace, friend.''

Abigail bit her lip. This was no time for tears. She should be happy the tribe seemed ready to welcome Elijah and her. From what she could see, the tribe seemed to be prospering. So why did her heart feel so heavy?

''Let us go,'' Rani said. ''My husband is probably pacing, wondering what happened to me.''

Her friend's prediction proved to be true. Tracker, a name that Abigail gave him years ago, was walking around a tree, and Elijah was leaning against the trunk, watching the young man. Elijah was the first one to spot them. He pushed away from the tree and his gaze locked with Abigail's. His look was so intense that it could have melted steel. Abigail glanced down at the top of her dress to make sure everything was all right. Surely Elijah's gaze was prompted by something unusual.

Apparently his actions brought Tracker to a halt. He exchanged words with Rani, but Abigail only heard them distantly. She was in another world, inhabited by two people, Elijah and her.

Elijah had the sarong wrapped around his waist, in the traditional fashion. He was barefoot, bare-chested, and had a lei of tree leaves around his neck, which all the men wore. His chest was well muscled, his belly washboard hard. A light sprinkling of hair dusted across his pecs and narrowed down to his stomach. A shock so strong that Abigail was surprised she didn't burst into flames raced along her nerves.

His gaze locked with hers. Judging from the fire in his expression, apparently her appearance had a similar effect on him.

The corner of his generous mouth kicked up. "You look very becoming in that, Abigail. But there's no way I would mistake you for a native." His fingers picked up several strands of her blond hair that rested on her breast. "The color is a dead giveaway." She felt as if he'd snatched the air from her lungs.

"When I was a kid, I hated the color." She said the first thing that popped into her head. "I stood out like a sore thumb among the other children. And my skin burned easily. Finally, the others took pity on me and showed me how to avoid being baked like a lobster. I spent more time than I can count with mud smeared on my face, arms and legs, trying to hide from the sun." She took a deep, shuddering breath. "I just wanted to be one of the kids. Not a freak."

He tucked her hair behind her shoulder, his fingers grazing the soft skin. Heat and electricity danced down her arm and across her breasts. Her gaze fastened on his again. Her own turmoil was reflected in the depths of his brown eyes. She looked away, unable to continue to face the attraction she saw there.

They were both in this situation because they had no choice, she sternly warned herself. This attraction that had sparked to life needed to be ignored so they could go on.

"I wish I could've seen you smeared with mud." There was a laugh in his voice.

"I was skinny, with what I thought were big ears and a big mouth."

Elijah's gaze moved to her lips. His finger touched the lower lip that seemed to pout. "Oh, no, that mouth of yours is perfect."

Abigail nearly melted from the heat. The heat in his eyes, the warmth radiating from his body.

Someone cleared his throat. Abigail looked away, suddenly aware that they were back on planet Earth, with an audience in attendance.

"We will be late if we do not go now," Tracker said in English, frowning at Elijah and Abigail.

His wife nudged him. "They will follow."

"What?" Tracker said, holding up his hands.

Rani simply gave him a look that said she'd tell him later.

When Abigail glanced back at Elijah, he was staring off into the distance, a slight color tinting his cheeks.

A smile curved her lips. Whoever would have thought that Elijah Kendrick, super spy, knew how to blush?

Finally, he glanced back at her. "We'd better catch up with Rani and Tracker before they send out a search party for us."

They followed the other couple through the village to the central area where everyone gathered for the meal. Samuel and his family were sitting in the circle in a spot of honor. He motioned to Abigail and Elijah to come and sit with them.

Once they had made their way through the crowd,

Samuel stood up and motioned for everyone to be quiet.

"My friends, I wish to introduce you to Abigail McGee Kendrick, the daughter of our good friends and teachers, David and Lisa McGee." Samuel spoke in the native dialect. "By her side is her husband, Elijah. After our feast, Abigail wishes to address us."

Abigail and Elijah bowed to the group, then sat down. Samuel prayed over the dinner, then motioned for the servers to bring in the food.

"Elijah, that is a very Biblical name," the Indian sitting next to Elijah said in English. "Were your parents missionaries also?" he asked.

Elijah choked on his drink, bringing everyone's attention to him. The Indian patted Elijah on the back and Abigail leaned toward him.

"Are you all right?" she asked him.

He tried to speak, but for a moment speech seemed beyond him. Elijah simply nodded. Finally, he turned to the Indian. "My father was a farmer."

"I meant no offense. Forgive me for asking. I thought since you are married to Abigail and have such a strong name, that your parents might have walked as Abigail's did."

An easy smile curved Elijah's lips. "I completely understand. No offense was taken."

The Indian nodded and turned to his family.

After a moment, Elijah asked, "What did Samuel say?"

"He introduced us. Our time to speak will be at the end of the meal."

Several of the village women stopped in front of them with large platters of food. On the first were cooked vegetables and bread. The second held fish and some sort of meat.

"What is that?" Elijah whispered in Abigail's ear. He was pointing to the meat on the platter.

"It's tasty and very unusual."

"But what is it?" he persisted.

"Trust me, Elijah, you'd prefer not to know."

"I've roasted a rat and eaten it when there was nothing else."

Abigail's brow arched. "Then you'll not be bothered by eating that."

"Still not going to tell me, huh?"

"It a capybara."

"Capybara?"

"An Amazon rodent."

He took the meat from the platter and bit into the fried chunk. "It's not bad." He noticed she hadn't taken a piece. "Aren't you going to have any?"

She shook her head. "Nope."

Abigail was surprised by how well Elijah dealt with the villagers. He seemed at ease with them, exchanging nods with the men and smiles with the children.

When the women came around for a final time with fruit, Samuel stood up.

"My friends, Abigail wishes to speak to you." He motioned for her to stand and deliver her request.

As she stood, Elijah offered her his arm. When she gained her feet, he lightly squeezed her hand, as if silently telling her he was with her. He sat back down. Abigail motioned to Rani, then quietly asked her to interpret her words for Elijah. Rani nodded and sat next to him.

Abigail licked her dry lips as she looked around at

the faces she thought never to see again in this lifetime. A dozen memories crowded her brain.

"I am very honored to be here tonight," she said in the native tongue. "I see many faces that I recognize. Others are not here, but I keep them close to my heart. They shall always be with me."

She took a deep breath to steady herself, and felt Elijah slide his hand around her ankle. She glanced down at him and saw the sea of calm in his eyes. It was as if he pulled her to himself and shared with her his well of tranquillity.

She faced the crowd. "I will tell you that my heart was wounded when my parents died and I chose not to remember this place and you. That was wrong. But heaven must be looking out for me because Elijah was sent to me." She paused and looked at Elijah. His face didn't reflect his surprise at her words, but she'd bet her Elvis collection that her words had surprised him.

"Two nights ago," she continued, "a plane from my country went down in the jungle close to you. Samuel told me of the young men of this village who went out yesterday morning to find this plane and have not returned.

"We need your help to save the people on the plane. I ask now for that. Elijah has brought with him a machine that hears the beep the airplane makes. We need volunteers to help us."

Every man in the village stood. Although none of the women did, Abigail knew that it was tribal custom that prevented them from going on such an adventure.

Tears streamed down Abigail's cheeks. "Thank you, my friends."

For the next few minutes, it seemed that everyone

in the village came by and greeted her and Elijah. Each shared a story of her parents with them. Rani continued to interpret for Elijah. Abigail held Elijah's hand. He stood beside her and his arm slipped around her waist to draw her to his side. She leaned into him.

By the time the last group of people had talked with them, Abigail's heart was so full that she battled tears. Emotionally exhausted, she slumped against Elijah.

"Is anything wrong?" he softly asked.

"No." It was a pitiful sound, unconvincing in its tone. She'd already bawled once today and was determined not to do it again. For years she hadn't cried over her parents' fate. Instead, she had placed her feelings behind a wall and carefully cemented them away. Now it seemed the wall was crumbling, leaving those feelings raw and in full view.

"When we deny our heart its sorrow, it sometimes makes us pay dearly for our mistake," Rani explained to Elijah as he stared at Abigail. "Abigail's heart is now talking. It has been silent too long."

Abigail looked at Rani.

"Listen to it, friend. You have ignored it too long. Now is the time to be whole." She kissed Abigail on both cheeks.

Abigail's knees gave out on her. Elijah scooped her up in his arms and walked back to their hut, hoping that some idea on how to comfort her would occur to him.

What did he know about dealing with females? What did he know about dealing with grief? His parents had been poor farmers in rural Oklahoma, just eking out an existence. His mother had hated life on the farm, and one day went to get groceries in the nearby city and never returned home. His father had taken to the bottle afterward, moaning that he'd failed. When Elijah and his sister, May, were eight and six, his father had fallen off the tractor in a drunken haze and broken his neck. That day, after the cops had left, Social Services had come for him and his sister. He hadn't been any help to May then, couldn't comfort her tears when she'd been taken and assigned to a different family from the one who kept him. He knew then he was a failure with emotional things. He had locked away his feelings, unwilling to let them surface again and put him through that torture.

Since he'd seen his father's self-destruction, Elijah had carefully avoided giving his heart. His college sweetheart had once called him a cold, unfeeling bastard. She'd been right on the mark.

Unfortunately, all the rules that had been in place in his life up to now seemed to be turned on their head, leaving him without a clue how to act.

Chapter 6

Elijah felt the eyes of all the villagers on him as he carried Abigail back to their hut.

"You can put me down," she whispered into his neck, her warm breath skimming over his skin, raising feelings that he had no business experiencing.

He keenly felt the weight of her against him. Since he was bare to the waist, Abigail's cheek rested on his shoulder, and the soft skin of her shoulders was warm against his. He kept walking and didn't respond to her comment.

"I can walk, Elijah," she said again, her head coming off his shoulder.

He looked into her eyes. "I know you can. But I think everyone expects me to carry you."

"Oh." She sounded disappointed that he didn't have nobler motives for his actions.

Well, hell, he thought, clenching his teeth. She'd be truly shocked to know that his thoughts were traveling in a much more basic and primitive direction. From the looks several of the men were giving him, they knew what was in his head.

He didn't need this complication. He had an agent out in the jungle who probably needed care, another search team with unclear motives moving toward them, a mole in Washington, and what was he doing? Panting after Abigail like an adolescent. Where was his renowned cool and detached manner? It seemed to evaporate the minute he laid eyes on Abigail.

Damn, but she felt right, cuddled up against his chest. Her breasts were pressed against him, making him want to touch them, explore their fullness. His other hand was hooked under her knees. The cloth of her skirt didn't cover the skin of her thighs where his hand was. Her skin was soft and smooth, making him want to slide his hand up and down her legs. And do other things.

He carried her to their hut, opened the door and walked inside. He released her knees, allowing her body to slide slowly down his. It was torture, making him grind his teeth against the wave of want that washed over him.

She looked up into his eyes, hers bright with tears and sorrow. What a rotten time for him to be feeling this way. He couldn't give in to his hormones now.

Secrets that the government held were being sold to the highest bidder and needed to be stopped. And what was he doing? He was thinking with his zipper.

Elijah took a deep breath, fighting to bring himself back under control. He hadn't had this much trouble with his libido since he was sixteen. His body wasn't paying attention to his mind. "Your speech to the villagers was very effective. We'll have plenty of volunteers to go with us tomorrow morning.''

"Don't credit me. The villagers are the ones who deserve it.''

What haunted him from her speech to the Indians was the pain he saw in her eyes. It had struck him then that this trip was costing her a lot in emotional tender. She was paying for their success with her heart. He felt guilty. And he didn't like it one bit.

He started to open his mouth when a knock sounded on the door. He opened it and saw Tracker on the other side. In his hands were Elijah's regular clothes and shoes.

"I need to talk to you about tomorrow morning," Tracker said as he handed Elijah his clothes.

Elijah was grateful for the other man's timely interference. He glanced over his shoulder. "I'll be back in a few minutes," he told Abigail. He noticed the relief in her eyes.

She nodded.

He turned to Tracker. "Why don't we walk?"

"Of course."

They walked to the edge of the village, where Tracker's hut was located. "How do you want to organize things tomorrow morning?"

"Have everyone gather at the eating area at sunrise," Elijah said. "I have the homing device. I'll take it with us."

"Maybe we will meet the men we sent out yesterday. It will make things easier for all."

For a moment, Elijah had forgotten about the search group. "I hope our luck is running that way." But Elijah didn't have confidence it would. Too many things hadn't gone as he expected since the mission started.

"Then, we will meet tomorrow morning after breakfasting. Good night," Tracker said.

Elijah watched Tracker walk away. His gaze scanned the village. Most of the residents had gone to bed. The place looked prosperous, the children well tended, and everyone appeared healthy. It seemed that progress hadn't hurt this particular village. Or maybe they had fought hard against the encroachment of the twentieth century.

Elijah glanced down at the clothes he held in his hands. He'd better change out of his native "outfit" before he returned to Abigail. He stepped into the jungle and quickly put on his regular clothes. He folded the cloth he wore and carried it under his arm.

He knocked on the door frame and waited for Abigail's okay to enter. When she replied, he pushed open the door. She had changed back into her own clothes just as he had. The sleeping mat that the Indians used was unrolled and in the middle of the room.

"I hope that mat is more comfortable than it looks. I'm sore from sleeping on the ground last night." He shook his head. "I guess I'm getting too old for this kind of stuff."

She studied him. "It's got nothing to do with your age. It's what you're used to."

"Then I guess I've gotten spoiled over the last few years." He shook his head. "I remember a time when…"

"When what?" She sounded desperate to talk. He guessed she wanted to divert her mind from the memories assailing her.

He flashed her an aw-shucks-madam-I-can't-talk-about-that smile. "Even though we are married, I can't talk about some things." He meant it teasingly. It came out in an entirely different way, reminding them both of what this trip had already cost them.

Abigail's eyes darkened, and she turned away and took a deep breath. "It's been a long day. And to-morrow will be an even longer one. We'd best go to sleep." She sat on the mat and lay down.

He had successfully put an end to the conversation with the finesse of a three-legged bull. "No blanket or pillows?" he asked.

She pointed to the side of the hut where their luggage and packs were stacked. "There are some more mats over there. Fold one up and use it as a pillow. As for a blanket—" She let the remainder of the sentence hang. There was no need for a blanket in this weather. A fan, yes. A blanket, no.

He followed her instructions, but what he ended up with was worse than going without. He pushed away the mat and stared up at the ceiling.

Out of nowhere the thought occurred to him that this wasn't what Abigail had expected her wedding night to be like. It certainly wasn't the hearts and roses most young women imagine for their honeymoon. And if he had planned on having a wedding night—which he hadn't, since he hadn't planned on getting married—this definitely wouldn't be it. A chuckle escaped his mouth.

Abigail turned her head toward him. There was a question in her eyes about what he found so funny.

He intended not to answer her, but she rose on her elbow. "What is it? I certainly could use a laugh."

"I know this isn't exactly what you dreamt your wedding night would be like."

"Oh."

Apparently his meaning was crystal clear to her, and he saw her blush. "Go to sleep, Abigail. It's been a long, eventful day."

She saw the airplane explode, bursting into flames. Pieces of the wreckage fell to the earth in a fiery shower.

"No," Abigail shouted, reaching out, trying to stop what she knew was going to happen. Her eyes flew open and she jerked to a sitting position.

She looked around wildly, trying to orient herself after the wrenching nightmare.

A large hand settled on her back, then she felt the warmth of Elijah's breath on her neck. "Abigail, what's wrong?"

He didn't seem the least bit sleepy. He sounded in full control of his senses.

She glanced over her shoulder at him. His gaze was sharp and probing. "A nightmare?" he asked.

"Yes." A shudder ran through her.

His hand rubbed over her back. "C'mon, Abby, lie down. You're going to need your strength."

She didn't want to go back to sleep. "I'm fine. I'll just sit up."

His hand grasped her chin, and he brought her face around to his. "No, you won't. I can still see the fatigue on your face. And you're not going to be any use to me or those men on the plane if you can't function tomorrow."

"Samuel can help you with the Indians," she answered, pulling her chin out of his grasp.

"Oh, did I miss something? When did he go to nursing school?"

She glared at him, unable to answer. If there were injuries, which were likely, and the people needed medical attention, it would be better if a nurse was in the rescue team.

"I didn't think so." His finger brushed back a lock of hair that caught on her eyelashes. He slid his hand up her back and cupped her shoulder. "Lie back down with me, Abby."

He didn't give her an opportunity to protest, but stretched out, taking her with him. His arms didn't release her once they were prone. Instead, he settled her more comfortably against his side.

His nearness certainly smashed the remnants of her nightmare. But now her body was humming to a different tune.

"Relax," he commanded softly.

Oh, fine thing for him to say, she thought sourly. She leaned her head back and started to snap at him, but there was something, some feeling, some understanding in his gaze that reached out to her. She sighed and rested her head on his shoulder. His hand lightly rubbed her upper arm.

"I used to have nightmares about Social Services taking my sister, May, and me away from the farm. I would dream that my dad was still alive and my mom hadn't deserted us. Then they would both disappear and it would rip my guts out when Social Services would come and take us away." He fell silent.

She looked up at him. He seemed disgruntled by his words. His revelation showed him in a different light than she was used to seeing him. She could picture the vulnerable child he'd been. "How did you deal with the fear and anger that the dreams brought?'' She didn't doubt that he'd had nightmares.

''I worked so hard during the day that at night I would fall into a dreamless sleep.'' He shrugged. ''It usually worked.''

There was a wealth of pain in his words. She wanted to ask more questions, but from his expression, she could see he wouldn't answer.

''You're not relaxing, Abby,'' he commented, stating the obvious.

''How observant,'' she grumbled to herself.

''Why don't you tell me about your life here?''

He'd hit her problem smack on the head. She didn't want to remember her time here. Facing the good things her parents did and how they touched the people would destroy the wall of resentment that she had built up over the years. If they had done such a wonderful job, then why did they have to die? Logically she knew one had nothing to do with the other, but logic didn't have anything to do with her feelings.

''You know about me from my file,'' she began. ''But I don't know anything about you. Tell me about yourself.''

She felt his body still. ''What do you want to know?''

She turned the question over in her mind. What did she want to know about this mysterious, attractive man? What would he answer? Nothing personal. ''How did you join the CIA? Was it always your ambition when you were growing up?''

He laughed, a deep, rich sound that set up a longing in her heart. ''My main ambition when I was growing up was to make it through another day.''

She leaned back, wanting to see his eyes, wanting

to know what he meant. His gaze was far away, seeing images that she could only guess at.

"I was a runner in high school. It got me a scholarship to OU." He glanced down at her. "It was my senior year, I was a business major. There were signs on campus that the CIA was going to be conducting job interviews at the psych building. Anyone interested was to come by. On a lark, I went."

"They obviously thought you were a good candidate."

He shrugged. "What can I say? I was intrigued."

"And you went to work for them when you graduated from college?"

"No. I joined the army, and that's where I was introduced to military intelligence. I loved the work, found out that I was good at it. When my hitch was over, I applied to the CIA, and the rest, as they say, is history."

He wasn't exactly chatty. She'd have to drag every bit of information out of him.

"How did you get the name Elijah?" The question popped out, startling her as much as him.

"My mother liked it."

Abigail rolled her eyes. "Didn't she ever tell you why she liked the name?"

"I don't remember too much about her. She left us when my sister and I were young."

Her brows furrowed into a frown. "She deserted you?"

He met her eyes. There was a starkness in his voice that spoke volumes about his life. "My mother split. She didn't like the life of a poor farmer in rural Oklahoma, so she left me, my sister and dad. She never contacted us again."

His pain sliced through her heart. Unable to ignore his suffering, she wrapped her arm around his waist and couldn't prevent herself from hugging him.

"Now, I don't know if she's still living or dead," he quietly added. "And I don't care."

She didn't believe him for a moment. His voice was too stark for him not to care. She was sorry she'd asked the question, bringing the painful time back to him.

"Your memories of your parents might be bitter-sweet," he whispered, his fingers sifting through her hair, "but be grateful. Mine are only bitter."

She couldn't say anything in response to his comment. He was right. There had been tragedy in her life, but it had been a good life with loving parents and warm memories. Apparently Elijah had not been so fortunate.

"I'm sorry," she murmured, her lips moving against his shoulder.

His hand brushed her hair back from her face. "Don't be. What I went through made me strong."

She closed her eyes and listened to the beat of his heart. No, what he had gone through had robbed him of his childhood, and his trust in others. She understood why he was so good at his job.

"Go to sleep, Abigail. The morning will be here soon."

She closed her eyes, her heart aching for him.

Elijah didn't know what insane impulse had possessed him to tell Abigail about his childhood. He hadn't thought about his mother in years. He'd been tempted several times to try to find her. Having access to all that government information, it wasn't too hard to track her down. One year just before Christmas he gave in to the gnawing that had wrenched his soul for so long. He found his mother in Chicago, a hollowed-out shell of a woman who was living with a man. When he approached her and identified himself, she turned away. Never said hello, I'm sorry for deserting you, forgive me, drop dead. Just an empty-eyed look. That was enough for Elijah. Never again had he wondered about her. Over the years, he'd kept in contact with his sister, but he never told her about their mother and his meeting with her. May's adoptive parents were good people, and Elijah had no desire to bring that painful memory back to his sister.

So why had he spilled his guts to Abigail? No, he really hadn't spilled his guts, telling her all the ugly details of his life. It just felt that way. He'd told her more about his past than he'd ever shared with another individual.

He buried his face in the softness of her hair. The light floral scent of her shampoo still lingered, making his fingers itch to bury themselves in the thick richness, pulling her head back for his kiss.

He wanted to do other things. He felt every inch of her shapely form against his. He knew she needed the comfort of a warm body after she woke from her nightmare, and he couldn't turn away from that need. He remembered how his sister would wake, crying for their mother after the woman had deserted them. Although he couldn't make May's pain go away, he'd held her while she cried.

So now he'd created his own hell. His body wanted this woman in his arms. His head told him Abigail didn't want him, she simply wanted some comfort. And yet he remembered the desire he'd seen in her eyes.

He gritted his teeth. *Go to sleep,* he counseled himself. No matter how much he wanted to make love to her, he couldn't. Making love to her would be unwise. He wasn't cut out for marriage. If he wanted to get an annulment when they went back to the States, then he had to keep his hands to himself.

But...

Sleep was a long time in coming.

Elijah gently shook Abigail awake.

"It's time to get up," he told her.

Her eyes fluttered open, her gaze soft with sleep. Automatically, her lips curved into a smile. "Good morning," she murmured sleepily.

Another scenario popped into Elijah's mind, making him grit his teeth. She was tearing out his gut. "We're going to leave as soon as it's light. You have about five minutes to change and get outside."

She wrapped her arms around her upraised knees. Her blond hair fell around her shoulders like a curtain. "Do you think you could find me a cup of coffee?" she asked, combing her fingers through her hair.

"We're in Brazil, Abigail. Why wouldn't there be coffee here?"

"Because, when we lived here years ago, the evil of coffee hadn't invaded the village. Although my parents drank it, the villagers didn't like its taste."

"But you fell for its siren song?" he teased.

Her gaze flew to his. She couldn't stop the smile bursting through her reserves. "It's one of my weaknesses."

"You have others?" His brow arched.

Her eyes reflected her surprise that he was teasing her. It was hard for him to believe it, himself.

"Yes," she whispered.

His eyes narrowed. "I'd like to know what those are, but we need to leave as soon as possible. I'll knock before I come back in."

It took him a moment for his mind to focus on what he needed to do. He walked to the center of the village where all the cooking was done. He saw Tracker there with several of the volunteers.

"Good morning," he called out.

Tracker stood. "How is Abigail this morning?"

"She is fine, but she sent me looking for a cup of coffee. Is there any around here?" Elijah asked.

Pointing to Samuel's hut, Tracker said, "I'm sure Maya has made coffee for Samuel and will give you a cup for your wife."

The word *wife* seemed to grab his heart and squeeze. Elijah nodded. He walked toward Samuel's hut. Outside, on an open fire, Maya was cooking. An enamel pot hung over her cook fire.

"Good morning, Maya," Elijah greeted the woman.

She glanced up from her skillet and nodded.

"Abigail sent me looking for a cup of coffee."

Smiling, Maya nodded toward the cups set out. "If you get a cup, I will pour some for her. If you want some yourself, get another cup."

Elijah grabbed two cups. The smell as Maya poured the liquid made his mouth water. "I can see why Abigail is so hooked on this stuff."

"Are you hungry?" Maya asked. "You and Abigail will need a good meal before you start off into the jungle. I will serve you some of this meat and yams while you get your wife."

He didn't want to waste the time to eat. He wanted

to be out in the jungle and beat the other team looking for the plane, but it was foolish to start off without some nourishment. Nodding, he went back to their hut.

"Abigail," he called when he was outside their hut. He waited a moment, then she opened the door and he moved into the room. She had plaited her hair into a single braid that fell well past her shoulder blades. Her face broke into a smile when she spotted the cup in his hand. Immediately, she took it from him and sipped the rich liquid. Her eyes fluttered closed in enjoyment.

His gut tightened in reaction to the look of ecstasy on her face. He wouldn't mind being the one that placed that expression there. He cursed under his breath. He didn't need this grief.

"Maya has breakfast ready for us," he said, trying not to think about the look of pleasure on her face.

She took another swallow, pausing to enjoy the flavor on her tongue. After savoring the richness, she said, "I'm ready."

He grabbed the beacon receiver, then opened the door for her, following her out into the sunlight. He was surprised to find the sun shining as brightly as it was. "What happened to sunrise?" he asked, looking around.

"It's hard to get used to, isn't it?"

"What?"

"One minute it's dark, and the next instant it's light. Here near the equator, there is no such thing as a prolonged sunrise and sunset, where the sky is colored with the sun's rays. When my family moved back to the States, sunrise and twilight fascinated me. I could never get used to the colors, and how the sky would change from orange to purple to black, or vice versa.''

He'd never thought about sunsets before. He'd certainly never stood around watching the colors of the sky. There were more important things to do, like surviving.

"And the other thing I found so strange when we moved back to the States was rain.''

"Rain?'' He stopped and stared at her. "Rain is the same here in the jungle or in the States. It's wet.''

She shook her head. "You don't understand. Mom and Dad moved to Denver after we lived here. In Denver when it rains, you can smell it. It's a wonderful smell, fresh and clean. Here in the jungle, it's so humid that you can't smell it. In Denver the humidity is so low that the rain makes a difference.''

He'd never thought about rain, except that it was wet. He remembered back to his childhood, and tried to remember if the rain had a smell. What the rain had meant to him and his father was that the crops would grow. That was what was important about rain.

Seeing it through her eyes was a unique experience.

When they arrived back at the center of the village, Maya had already served them portions for breakfast.

"Good morning, Abigail,'' Maya greeted. "How did you sleep last night?''

Abigail's gaze met Elijah's. He could see she was remembering how they'd spent most of the night in each other's arms.

"I slept well, Maya,'' Abigail replied, taking a plate from her and settling down beside the other woman. Elijah settled next to Abigail, took his plate and began to eat.

"Is Samuel going to come with us?" Abigail asked.

Maya shook her head. "No. He'll stay here."

By the time they finished eating, the other Indians who'd volunteered had joined them in the clearing. Elijah explained to Tracker how the beacon finder worked, then turned it on. On their way out of the village, they stopped by their hut and gathered the medical supplies and radio that Elijah and Abigail had brought with them.

Tracker led the way with Elijah behind him, holding the beacon finder. The others followed, hacking back the vegetation from the seldom-used path. They had been out in the jungle for about a half hour when they ran into the group of Indians sent out two days before. They had been unable to locate the plane.

The beacon locator indicated that the plane was in a ninety degree direction from where they had searched.

They went west, toward the mountains.

Around noon, the first of the wreckage was spotted. The plane had slammed into the towering peak that rose above the jungle floor. The wreckage was sitting halfway up the slope. The wings had broken off the fuselage and the main body of the plane was ripped into two major sections. The nose was up on a jutting part of the peak. The main part of the cabin had slipped down beneath, tearing a path down the mountain.

It took the rescue party almost an hour to climb up to where most of the airplane rested.

Elijah looked into the open neck of the airplane. There were eight people strapped into their seats. He quickly determined only one of the men was alive, his agent. Immediately, Abigail began to work on the injured man.

"I'll see if anyone in the other part of the airplane above us is alive," Tracker informed Elijah.

Elijah nodded his consent, then turned back to watch Abigail stabilize his friend.

"Can you unlock the briefcase from his wrist?" Abigail asked.

Elijah found the key on a chain around Jerry's neck and unlocked the handcuffs that held it on his wrist.

"No," the man protested.

"It's okay, Jerry," Elijah said to the man, glad that his friend had spoken.

Jerry's eyes opened, and he tried to focus on Elijah. "You got the papers?" he asked.

"Yeah, Jer, I've got the papers."

"Good," he breathed.

Abigail began an IV on the man. Jerry was drifting in and out of consciousness.

"I never would've believed it," Jerry babbled. He grasped Elijah's hand.

"What, Jer? What is it that you wouldn't have believed."

"The papers. They tell who the mole is."

Elijah breathed a sigh of relief that the goal of Jerry's mission had been completed.

"I'll bet you'll never guess who it is," Jerry whispered.

"Who is it?"

Jerry closed his eyes. "Neil."

Elijah couldn't believe his ears. "Say it again, Jer."

Jerry didn't answer. He had passed out.

Since Elijah didn't know the combination on the

briefcase lock, he glanced around the destroyed cabin and found a piece of steel. He used it to pry apart the lock, opened the briefcase and pulled out the papers that were inside. Glancing through them, he looked for the name of the traitor. On the next-to-last page, he found the name.

Neil Teatly. His boss.

Chapter 7

Elijah stared down at the sheet of paper. No matter how hard he looked, the name didn't change.

Neil Teatly. His boss. Friend. Mentor. Traitor.

A searing pain ripped through his chest, and Elijah glanced down to see if someone had actually shot him. No. There was no visible wound. But there was a gaping wound inside, from which he was bleeding.

He felt that hours had passed, the feeling of betrayal was so acute. He glanced over at Abigail who was securing the IV line in Jerry's arm. Only a few seconds had actually gone by, but it felt like more to Elijah.

Slipping the papers back into the briefcase and closing it, Elijah walked over to Abigail. "How's Jerry?" He needed to focus on something besides the pain inside him.

"Pretty banged up. I think there are some internal

injuries. We need to get him to a hospital as soon as possible. They've been without help too long."

Tracker appeared at the open end of the fuselage. "The pilot's alive, but Molei, who found him, thinks the pilot's leg and arms are broken."

Abigail glanced up. "I'm almost done here. All I need to do is finish this dressing on his leg."

"I'll do that," Elijah said.

She gave him a skeptical look.

"Ye of little faith," he whispered as he took the gauze from her hands.

"It's not that I don't trust you, it's just—"

Elijah laid a finger over her lips. "Sh. Don't worry about it. I've been given medical training for emergencies. This, I think, qualifies as an emergency."

She thoughtfully considered his words, then nodded.

"Let me gather my supplies and I'll follow Molei up the mountain."

After repacking her medical supplies in her backpack, Abigail headed after the Indian. Elijah worked on his friend and finished wrapping the dressing on his leg. Thankfully, Jerry was unconscious.

Elijah tried hard to keep his mind on what he was doing, but little things popped into his head, like the first time he'd met Neil on the college campus. Or the day he graduated from training school and Neil had been there, the only person who'd been personally interested in how he'd done.

As he fought the memories, it seemed that the wound in his chest grew worse. He took a deep breath and walked to the open end of the plane and looked up the mountain. Molei and Tracker appeared out of the nose of the plane carrying a stretcher they'd made from some of the downed trees and rope they'd found in the plane. Abigail followed behind them.

"How is he?" Elijah asked as soon as she reached him.

"The pilot's injuries are as bad as Tracker said. Both of his arms and one leg are broken in several places. Fortunately for him, we found a piece of cabin flooring that was long enough to use as a backboard to immobilize his body, so if there are any spinal injuries, we haven't complicated them."

Tracker stopped in front of Elijah. "How is your friend?"

"According to Abigail, we need to get him to a hospital and fast."

"What do you wish to do now?" Tracker asked.

"We need to leave everything as it is. There is another group—an official government group coming to collect the wreckage. They will determine what caused this crash."

Tracker spoke to the men, instructing them to leave everything as it was.

"Do you wish for me to leave some men here to tell the other rescuers about the survivors?"

What Elijah needed most was a head start from the others searching for the plane. And time to sort out the mess he found himself in. "No. Abigail and I need time to bring the information we found back to the States. The cause of the wreck won't change, no matter how long it takes for the official rescue team to find it."

When they finally got the pilot down to the level of the fuselage, Abigail looked at the tall trees around them that covered the area. "Too bad we can't call in medical help here."

Elijah turned to Tracker. "Is there some place close where the trees thin out enough to land a helicopter?"

Tracker thought for a moment. "Yes. Two years ago when they were building the road through the jungle, a helicopter brought supplies to the men. It landed where the river that starts on this mountain joins the main body of the Majari. That triangle of land is clear of trees."

Abigail looked at Elijah. "I think it's the best chance these men have of surviving."

"All right, let's give it a try."

It took the better part of an hour to get the two men down the mountain.

As they walked to the spot in the jungle where the two rivers met, Tracker shook his head. "It is good that you are here, Abigail. Heaven must have sent you."

She turned to Elijah and gave him a knowing glance. Somehow Langley, Virginia, didn't seem like heaven to her, nor Elijah an angel of light.

His face was blank of all emotion, yet Abigail sensed a deep turmoil underneath the calm exterior. Why she felt that way, she couldn't say, but she couldn't shake the feeling. Something seemed to be bothering Elijah, and she didn't think it had anything to do with heaven. Maybe it had something to do with the briefcase he now carried.

When they reached the rivers' joining, Abigail checked her patients. Both men appeared to have endured the travel with surprising ease.

Immediately, Elijah radioed for help. Before he'd left Washington, D.C., he had contacted a pilot friend in Caracas and asked him to be on standby at a small airport on the Venezuelan-Brazilian border. Within moments, his friend was on the radio.

"Dave, I've got two seriously injured men who need immediate medical attention. Can you pick us up and transport us to the nearest hospital?"

"Sure. Give me your coordinates."

Elijah read off the coordinates on the GPS receiver that he'd carried with them.

"I'll be there within an hour, Elijah."

"We'll be waiting."

"What is that?" Tracker asked, pointing to the handheld instrument in Elijah's hand.

"It's called a GPS receiver or globe positioning system." Elijah pointed to the sky. "There is a satellite out in space that receives signals from this instrument and then tells the person holding it his exact location using longitude and latitude. I could tell the man flying the helicopter exactly where I was in the jungle."

Tracker nodded. "You must never get lost if you have this wonderful thing."

"If I have it with me, no, I don't get lost."

It turned out that it took only forty-three minutes for Dave to fly to their location. He landed the helicopter on the piece of land between the two rivers.

After they secured the injured men on the helicopter, Abigail smiled at each of the Indians and thanked them in their native dialect for their help. When she came to Tracker, her smile became wobbly. "We must go to help these men."

Tracker nodded. "I understand."

"Tell Rani I promise to write. Also please tell Samuel and Maya my heart is full of love for them."

"Will you return again someday?" Tracker asked.

She swallowed hard. "I cannot say. But I promise never again to forget my friends." She shook his hand. "Goodbye."

She climbed into the back seat of the helicopter.

"My thanks also," Elijah added. After waving to the Indians, Elijah hopped into the front seat and the helicopter took off.

"Tell me the condition of your patients," Dave said into the microphone of his headset once they were airborne.

Abigail heard the question on her headset. "Jerry has had some major trauma to his chest. He has a head injury and a deep wound on his leg. There are signs that he's in shock. He needs a hospital fast. The pilot has broken arms and a leg and a lump on his temple that needs to be looked at."

"The nearest hospital that would be able to deal with the extent of these injuries is the Sisters of Mercy in Ciudad Bolívar, the capital of the Bolívar region of eastern Venezuela," Dave answered. "That meet with your approval, Elijah?"

"Sure, no problem." Elijah still sounded distracted and distant.

Dave glanced over his shoulder at Abigail. "I'm Dave Murphy."

"Abigail McGee."

"You work for Elijah?" Dave asked, glancing at his friend. Elijah didn't join the conversation.

"No."

Dave arched his brow, and he looked at Elijah.

"Elijah asked me to do this favor for him. Since I'm a nurse, I couldn't refuse to come in case there were injured people."

Dave glanced at Elijah. He pointed his thumb at

the man sitting next to him. "He's a pro at getting folks to cooperate."

Abigail couldn't see Elijah's eyes, but she watched his mouth turn down in a frown. "That's enough, Dave. Abigail isn't interested in Company business."

Dave glanced back at her. "Oh, I don't know. She's sure interested in something. If it isn't Company business, maybe it's you."

Abigail glared at the back of Dave's head, then checked her patients' vital signs again. Jerry's pressure had bottomed out.

"How much longer?" Abigail asked.

"Twenty minutes."

"Can we make it there any faster?"

"Why?" Dave asked.

"Jerry's vitals are crashing."

Elijah turned around. "Which means what?"

"It means Jerry's blood pressure is dropping and his pulse is up, which is a sure sign that there's internal bleeding of some sort. When we brought him down the mountain, we triggered something. Their bodies have done a marvelous job of keeping them alive up until now, but I think Jerry's just about run out of luck."

The hospital in Ciudad Bolívar had been built ten years previously. The instant they landed on the rooftop, medical personnel from the hospital took over and wheeled the men into trauma rooms. Abigail followed, giving the nurses the vitals on both men.

"Dave, thanks for the ride." Elijah grabbed the briefcase that Jerry had carried. "Are you going back to Caracas?"

He nodded.

"If anyone in the Company calls looking for me, you haven't seen me or the men you brought here."

Dave's eyes narrowed. "What's going on, Elijah?"

Elijah realized he needed Dave's help to cover his backside. He needed time to sort out what he was going to do. And the best way to buy that time was to give Dave a brief synopsis of what was going on. "You know that rumor that's been whispered about for the last few years, that there's a mole high up in the agency? I now have proof. One of those men you brought in got it. But I suspect our mole won't go quietly. I need some time to set the trap. Can you give me that?"

Dave studied him. "You think you have this guy nailed?"

"I think so."

"All right, if anyone calls, I won't say anything."

"Thanks." Elijah shook Dave's hand.

The hospital corridor seemed dark compared to the bright light of the afternoon. It took several minutes to find Abigail. She was sitting in the emergency waiting room. Elijah sat beside her, setting the briefcase between their chairs.

"How are things going? What happened with Jerry and the pilot?"

"They took both of them back into the trauma rooms. They'll X-ray the pilot to determine how extensive his injuries are. They probably took Jerry to surgery right away. They seem to be a very competent team. I'm impressed."

Ten minutes passed before the doctor came out into the waiting room. He addressed Abigail in Spanish. Finally the doctor pointed to him.

"What did he say?" Elijah asked.

"The pilot has lost a lot of blood because of the compound fractures. He needs to be stabilized before they can do surgery. Jerry has a concussion and a lacerated liver. He will need surgery right away to stop the bleeding. Will you sign a permission form for the men to have surgery?"

"Sure."

After the forms had been filled out, Abigail collapsed onto a chair and leaned her head back against the wall. Dark circles colored the skin under her eyes, and her fatigue seemed to settle on her like a cloak.

Elijah glanced at his watch and realized that it had been nearly twelve hours since they ate. Abigail had held up well under the circumstances. She hadn't complained about being hungry or tired or the miserable conditions of the trip.

"It's been a long day."

She nodded.

"Why don't we get something to eat? I don't think there's anything else we can do for those men."

She worried her bottom lip as she looked at the emergency room doors.

"I'm sure we could find you a good cup of coffee."

That brought a smile to her lips and a decision to her eyes. "Sure. Let me tell the nurse that we'll be back."

He closed his eyes and sighed. He felt like he'd been run over by a truck.

Neil was the traitor. The man who'd recruited him into the agency. The gung-ho guy who'd been a friend through the years. The man who'd gone out drinking with him after that fiasco when he tried to contact his mother.

"I warned the nurse we'd be gone for a while. I asked her for a good place to eat. She said there's a restaurant across the street from here that is excellent."

"Sounds good," he replied absently.

He didn't say anything while they walked to the restaurant. He carried the briefcase and set it under the table. Abigail interpreted the menu for Elijah. After they had ordered the evening special, Abigail crossed her arms under her breasts. "I take it whatever information you were after is in that briefcase that was handcuffed to Jerry's arm."

"Yes."

"And this information is bad news?"

From the no-nonsense look in her eyes, Elijah knew he would have to give her part of the truth. She deserved that, at least, because if he didn't miss his guess, she was in as much trouble as he. Lorenzo, the government official they'd met in Boa Vista, wouldn't waste any time reporting their activities to Neil. But now, in this public place, was not the time to discuss it. He purposely looked around at the other diners before he faced her again. "You did a good job with Jerry and the pilot." He hoped she realized why he was changing the subject.

She followed his lead and looked at the other diners. "Thank you. I'm persistent and thorough."

He read her warning clearly. He nodded in response. "It's always wise to be thorough."

He fingered the room-temperature soda bottle that the waiter had placed on the table. Before he could say anything else the waiter reappeared with their dinners.

It must've been the tone of his voice when he answered her, but she didn't ask any more questions for the rest of the meal.

Once they finished, they headed back to the hospital. The nurse informed them that Jerry had made it through surgery and would be in recovery for another hour at least. The pilot was stabilized and in surgery now.

"Jerry's doing well," Abigail told Elijah. A yawn caught her by surprise.

Her reaction reminded Elijah that when he swept down on Abigail, she had been up nearly thirty hours delivering a baby. She hadn't slept more than ten hours over the last couple of nights. She needed some rest. "Let's get a room and let you rest. I don't think we can do any more here."

"All right. Let me ask the nurse if she knows—"

He laid his hand on her arm. "No."

Her eyes widened. "Why?"

He retrieved the briefcase, took her arm and guided her down the hall. "Sometimes, Abigail, the fewer people who know where you are, the safer you are."

She regarded him warily. "Are you saying there's going to be trouble?"

He shrugged as they walked onto the elevator. "I've got a feeling, Abby, that before this is over, it's going to get dirty."

From her expression, his worry had come across loud and clear. Well, at least she had an accurate picture of what they were facing.

Across from the hospital were a string of medium-priced hotels that Elijah had noticed when they had gone to dinner. He liked the idea of staying close enough to the hospital to keep it under surveillance, although he didn't expect trouble, yet. It never paid to go into a situation blind, and Elijah was known for his attention to detail.

The first hotel they tried didn't have any vacancies. When Elijah requested a room, he spoke in perfect Spanish. A look of amazement colored Abigail's blue eyes, but she was smart enough not to question him in front of the hotel clerk.

Once they were out on the street, Abigail said, "I didn't think you knew Spanish."

"I don't. You heard the extent of my Spanish. I can ask for a room in seven different languages." He shrugged his shoulders. "It comes with the territory."

They tried the next hotel. It had several vacancies.

"*¿Prefieren Ustedes una habitación al lado de la calle o uno al lado del jardín?*" the clerk asked.

Elijah knew just enough Spanish to recognize the man was asking if they wanted a room by the street or garden. "*La calle.*"

The man nodded and gave them a key. "*Diez.*" He pointed overhead and toward the street, indicating where the room could be found.

Abigail and Elijah still had their backpacks with them, their only luggage besides the briefcase that contained the damning evidence. They walked up the stairs to the room at the front of the building. After unlocking the door, Elijah moved around the room, studying the view from the window. The front of the hospital was clearly visible.

"I guess it was kind of impractical to request two rooms?"

He threw her a dark look.

Abigail walked inside and sat down on the bed,

watching him. He waited for her to ask him what he was doing, but she remained silent.

Elijah went back out into the hall, then disappeared down the steps. He wanted to know the layout of the hotel. The entrances and exits. He discovered that the main door and a single door at the back were the only exit doors. Outside the corner room, which was next to theirs, he'd spotted a set of steel steps, the fire escape.

When he came back into the room, Abigail was still sitting on the bed. Her gaze narrowed. She seemed to be waiting, until finally she said, ''Tell me what's wrong, Elijah, and don't give me that CIA 'no comment' face of yours.''

Where was his famous poker face that showed no emotion, that everyone in the agency commented on? Why could this woman, who wasn't an expert in the art of deception, read him like a book?

Maybe she touched something in him that no other person had ever touched? a voice in his head whispered. He shook off the disturbing thought.

He ran his fingers through his hair, then rubbed them over his face. Unfortunately, Abigail was in the center of the mess, and she deserved to know what he suspected they were facing.

Tiredness pulled at him. He stretched out on the bed and stared at the ceiling. ''There are some things you need to know, Abby,'' he began.

She turned on the bed to face him. ''And what would that be?''

''As you know, Jerry was carrying some vital information.''

She didn't look duly impressed. ''And...''

''There's been someone inside the Company selling us out for a long time. Our agents in Russia were routinely discovered and shot. Eastern Europe also had a bad track record. Well, when the East German government fell, the Stazi—their CIA—seemed to vanish off the earth. Members have been slowly resurfacing all over the world with interesting information. One of the East Germans surfaced in Buenos Aires and contacted our embassy. He wanted money in exchange for the name of the mole. Jerry went there and met with the agent. He was provided with the agent's name and proof of the information he'd sold."

He paused, trying to figure the best way to tell her the rest.

"Why do I get this feeling that I'm not going to like what you're going to tell me?" A frown marred her brow.

His expression was serious. "That's because you're an unusually perceptive woman."

She snorted. "Don't dance around the issue, Elijah."

"I normally wouldn't tell you, but given the circumstances…" He sighed. "You'll need to be familiar with his name and what he looks like." It took him a moment to be able to say it. But finally he formed the words, "The mole is my boss, Neil Teatly."

She went white.

He pulled out his wallet, took out a picture and handed it to her. It was a Christmas photo of Elijah and a tall blond man. They were holding presents and grinning into the camera. "That's a picture of Neil. I want you to know what he looks like, just in case."

She frowned. "So what does this mean?"

"It means, Abigail, that until I can get hold of Neil's boss, things could get tough."

It didn't take her long. Her body immediately tensed. "You want to tell me what is going to happen?" The strained look on her face tugged at his heart.

He reached for her hand, lacing his fingers with hers. "I can't give you a certain scenario, Abby, but I can tell you what I think is going to go down."

She didn't answer but simply waited for him to continue.

"When Neil hears from our guy in Boa Vista, he's going to realize that I've managed to go in ahead of him. And that you're with me. When Neil discovers that I made it to the wreck first, he's going to float some sort of story trying to discredit me. It's what I would do in his place."

She handed back his wallet.

"I don't doubt there will be shoot-to-kill orders issued on me. You, being with me, will be in danger. You will be able to confirm my story, and Neil can't have that. He'll be after you, as well."

"Oh."

He was amazed at her bland reaction. He expected tears, maybe some yelling or cursing—no, she wouldn't curse. But he did expect a rather different reaction than a simple "oh." "Is that all you have to say?"

"What do you expect me to do?"

"Cry, scream, tell me I'm a bastard and it's my fault you're in this position."

There was a calmness about her that didn't seem natural. It was almost unearthly. "If I do any of that, will it make a difference?"

"No." He sat up on the bed, his frustration and fear for them riding him hard. "Sweetheart, maybe you don't understand. Your rear's in the sling along with mine."

That got a reaction. She jumped to her feet and glared at him. "I understand perfectly well that we're in trouble. But then, I knew you were trouble, Elijah, from the moment I saw you on my porch."

He cursed and stood up. She looked so beautiful, standing by the bed, her clothes wrinkled, her eyes reflecting the weariness that plagued them both. He couldn't face the fact that it was his fault that she was in this mess.

He opened his mouth to say something, then closed it because he couldn't trust himself to talk calmly with her. Where was the famous Elijah Kendrick control when he needed it? He took several deep breaths, then walked out of the room and climbed the stairs to the roof, where he would keep an eye on the hospital and the front door of the hotel while he wrestled with his guilt.

"Did you get to the plane first?"

"No. We arrived after Elijah and his group were there."

"What about the agent carrying the information?"

"There was no agent and no briefcase containing anything."

The first man cursed.

"There must have been survivors. As we were approaching the crash site, I heard a helicopter. I haven't sent out men to the local tribe. I'm sure they know what happened."

"Do what you have to do to keep the local authorities happy. If you pinpoint what happened to the survivors, let me know.''

When he hung up the phone, Neil looked out the window into the colorful autumn day. Slamming his palm down on the desk, he gritted his teeth. Dammit, if Elijah had that information, he'd take it straight to Terrence and unmask him as the mole.

Well, maybe he could cut Elijah off at the knees. What if he put out the story that the real mole was none other than Elijah, and that he'd gone on this mission to cover his tracks? That Elijah was simply pointing a finger at him to cast suspicion off himself.

That might work if the agent carrying the information was dead.

His fingers tapped a tattoo on the desktop. Therefore, he needed to find Jerry. What had Lorenzo said, a helicopter was heard close to the crash site?

Could it be one of theirs? He needed to go down to research and discover who they had in the area who flew choppers. Maybe he'd get lucky and find Jerry…and arrange another accident.

Her clothes stuck to her skin. And the dried sweat seemed to make everything worse. A shower is what she needed. Abigail pulled clean clothes from her backpack and picked up the towel and washcloth that were in the room. After locking the door, she went down the hall to the communal bathroom. The trickle of water was lukewarm, but it felt like heaven to Abigail.

She scrubbed her hair with the little bit of shampoo that she had in her travel-size bottle. When she toweled off minutes later, her frame of mind had improved considerably.

"Abby."

Her heart skipped a beat when she heard Elijah. She wrapped the towel around her. It didn't quite cover everything. "Yes," she called back through the wooden portal.

"You have the key to the room. I need it."

"Why couldn't you have picked the lock?" She bit her lip at the words that had popped out of her mouth. Why had she said that?

"Because the key was close, so why bother?"

He made sense. She grabbed the key and cracked open the bathroom door, thrusting it at him. "Here."

His gaze missed nothing, and suddenly there was a very definite kind of tension between them. All the times he'd held her close and kissed her over the last few days flashed through her brain. She felt blood rushing to her face as she slammed the door closed. Taking a deep breath, she tried to calm her racing heart. Her skin seemed extrasensitive as she slipped on her clothes. What was the matter with her that she was acting like a silly thirteen-year-old?

She laughed at the thought. What was the matter was a tall, brown-eyed man with a devastating smile who got to her like no other man she'd ever come in contact with. She bowed her head and rested her hands on the sink. What was she going to do? Worst of all, she suspected that Elijah felt something for her, and his feelings for her seemed to be as unwelcome as hers for him.

And how were they going to handle the sleeping arrangements tonight? The thought of spending another night in Elijah's arms certainly held a great deal of appeal—and danger. At this point, when nothing had happened between them, they could apply for an annulment. But if she continued on the road they were heading, then an annulment wouldn't be possible. A divorce—

Stop that, she chided herself. She was only borrowing trouble, and heaven knew that they had more than enough without adding to it.

Once she was dressed in clean clothes, she washed her dirty laundry out in the sink and folded it up in her towel.

When she got back to the room, she found Elijah in a chair, watching the hospital entrance. He glanced over his shoulder at her. There was still a spark of fire in his eyes.

"I want to go to the hospital and see how Jerry and the pilot are doing," he said.

"Fine." She hung her wet things over the knobs on the dresser. Elijah's gaze followed her movement. Her cheeks heated with embarrassment.

He stood and came up behind her. "Are you ready?"

She spun and faced him. "I hadn't planned on going with you."

Elijah grasped her chin in his fingers and brought her gaze up to his. "Until Neil is behind bars, Abby, you don't leave my side."

"But—"

He laid his fingers across her lips. It was like lightning striking her and racing through her body. Her eyes widened. His gaze focused on her mouth. He hovered over her, then muttered a curse and his lips settled on hers.

Suddenly the room disappeared, and all Abigail could feel was the warmth of his body enveloping hers. He smelled of sweat and sunshine and darkness and desire. And desperation. When he raised his head, she read in his gaze the scalding desire that was burning both of them. She held her breath, waiting for his next move.

Then his arms dropped away, and he took a step backward, a shuddering breath escaping his lips. "We'd better get going."

She could only nod her acceptance, because she knew if they stayed in this room, they would yield to the desire churning between them.

Chapter 8

The amount of traffic on the street at that time of night was amazing. Elijah and Abigail scurried between the cars and trucks, and reached the entrance of the hospital. They checked with the nurses in recovery and discovered that Jerry was in a private room and the pilot was still in recovery. They visited Jerry, only to find him asleep.

Elijah found himself wanting to wake the man and ask him how his meeting had gone with the East German rogue. He wanted to hear the details of the conversation. Abigail convinced him that nothing would be gained by trying to rouse Jerry.

She consulted the men's charts and informed Elijah that they were both out of the woods. With that reassurance, he escorted her back to the hotel room and took up his position by the window. After Abigail brushed her teeth, she lay down on the bed fully clothed.

"Are you expecting trouble?" she asked.

He glanced at her. "Not yet. But it always pays to be on guard."

She rose on her elbow. Her thick braid flowed over her shoulder, making him ache to run his fingers through the luxuriant mass. "Have you always been so distrustful, or is it something you've picked up spying?"

Her question made him think about his reaction. He guessed his actions spoke of distrust. They also spoke of knowing human nature and taking nothing for granted. The events of the last few days, learning how a friend could betray you, only reinforced his view. And his gut was yelling at him that things were going to get worse.

"My distrust comes from cold experience." His voice was ice hard.

Abigail's eyes grew dark with sadness. "I'm sorry, Elijah."

Her reaction truly stumped him. "For what?"

"For the hurt in your life that has given you such a cynical view of mankind."

He moved from the chair to the bed. His fingers smoothed the tendrils of hair that had escaped her braid. "It's no different than what a million others have experienced."

"That's where you're wrong. There is an entire world out there where love, loyalty, friendship are valued and treasured. Where friends can be trusted and a man's word is his bond. Where putting others first brings with it a joy that can be achieved no other way."

"If I had any doubt about who your parents were,

you just put them to rest.'' His hand dropped from her face and he turned.

She folded her legs under her. ''Elijah, your view of the world is colored by your work. You deal with the worst of mankind.''

He wanted to tell her that he'd learned his hard lessons years before as a child, deserted by his mother, then his father. But he didn't want to remind her of that. He didn't want her pity. Others had offered him their pity and it was bitter to swallow.

He turned back toward her, running his fingers over her cheek, feeling the smoothness of her skin. ''You're right. I see life through a jaundiced eye. But if I didn't, this world wouldn't be as safe. It's people like me who everyone depends on to keep the peace.''

As he started to draw his hand back, she caught it and held it against her cheek. ''No, that's not what we depend on. It's the nobleness of your heart, giving to others who don't know you're on the job. It's the best kind of action—selfless.''

Her words stopped him, his entire being stilled as he absorbed them. They were drink to his thirsty soul, food to his starved heart. Selfless, no. He was careful and never trusted in the nobler aspects of man. An individual had to prove to him through his actions that he was what he claimed to be. Seeing the world through Abigail's eyes showed him another aspect he'd never considered.

She turned her head and placed a kiss in his open palm, then looked into his eyes. In the depths of her blue ones, he saw admiration, respect, and something else. Something he didn't want to identify, didn't want to peg. Instead, his hand slipped behind her neck and drew her closer. Ever so slowly, he settled his mouth on hers. A moan escaped her and her eyes fluttered closed.

Blood pounded in his ears as his mouth devoured hers. She tasted better than the finest wine he'd ever had. And more satisfying.

Her arms wrapped around his waist, bringing her chest to his. He felt with every ounce of his being her breasts crushed against him. His hand slipped between their bodies and he covered one enticing mound, lightly squeezing.

All logical thought shut down for Elijah, and he acted purely on instinct. His fingers made quick work of his and Abigail's clothes; he wanted nothing to separate him from her.

Laying her on the bed, he feasted his eyes upon her smooth skin. When he joined her on the bed, his fingers released her hair from her braid. Lightly, he sifted through the strands. His mouth trailed down her cheek, to her neck where her pulse was pounding. Around her neck was a delicate chain, a small diamond resting in the notch at the base of her neck. He traced the links with his lips. Her hands skimmed up his back to anchor in his hair.

Each time his hand touched or stroked her and she responded, the fire inside him grew hotter, and the certainty that this was right strengthened. When at last he joined his body to hers, Elijah finally felt he'd come home.

"Are you all right?" he asked, having felt the evidence of her inexperience.

She nodded.

He wanted to question her more as to how she'd gotten to her age untouched, but Abigail began to move. All thoughts vanished and he could only feel.

He began to move, increasing the pace. She was with him, taking from him and giving back. They exploded, coming apart separately, but being reformed as one.

He rested his forehead on hers, trying to catch his breath after the incredible events of the last few minutes. Lightly, he brushed his mouth across hers. Her lips responded, sweetly clinging to his.

Rolling onto his side, he gathered her into his arms. He closed his eyes, savoring the feelings he'd just experienced. It had been fantastic. Great. The best he'd ever had. And he wanted to experience it again and again.

At the thought, a coldness swept over him.

He'd had sex with other women over the years. It was a pleasant diversion. A good feeling. But in the morning he'd always been able to say goodbye. This time, he didn't want to say goodbye. And that scared him spitless.

His dad had always wondered why his mom had left. His identity had been wrapped up in Elijah's mother, and without her, his dad had wasted away. That wasn't going to happen to him, he'd vowed to himself a long time ago.

Those ghosts riding him hard, Elijah pulled away from Abigail and slipped from the bed. She looked at him. It must've been the look in his eyes, but she clutched the sheet to her breast. He couldn't bear the confused look in her eyes. He grabbed his underwear.

"You were a virgin." He still couldn't believe it. "You were a virgin," he repeated, still stunned. "How does anyone in this day get to your age and still be a virgin? What were you saving it for?"

The instant the words were out of his mouth, he knew the answer to his question.

"I was saving 'it'—as you put it—for my husband, which, oddly enough…"

He cursed as he finished yanking on his clothes. With his guilt nearly choking him, he buttoned his shirt and pulled on his shoes. Unable to stay in this room a moment longer without saying something he might regret, he yanked open the door.

"Where are you going?" she asked.

"I'm going to check all the exits again, make sure everything is okay." It wasn't a lie. He'd check them all out. "I'll be back in a few minutes." Softly, he closed the door behind him. But he had the oddest feeling that it wouldn't be that simple to do with the emotions Abigail stirred in his heart.

Abigail pulled the sheet from the bed and wrapped it around herself. Gathering up her clothes, she opened the door to see if Elijah was still in the hall. It was empty. She rushed out of the room to the bathroom. Quickly, she was able to clean up and put on her clothes again.

Peering in the mirror, she wondered if she looked any different. It didn't appear so.

For a brief span of time, Elijah had let the walls down around his soul and allowed her in. It was a humbling yet glorious experience. Suddenly all those songs of love played on the radio made sense. This "feeling" compelled and made a person act.

She had purposely intended to wait until she found the man who would cherish her as her father had her mother. She had wanted her husband to be the first man. Oddly, Elijah fulfilled one of those requirements. He'd been her first lover, but she didn't fool herself that Elijah loved her as her father had her mother.

She thought about his reaction. At first, he'd appeared to be as affected by their loving as she had. Then abruptly, he'd pulled back. Why? Did he expect her to think this was a real marriage? It wasn't, no matter what passed between them.

Obviously, an annulment was now more difficult, that is, if they were honest. Elijah didn't deal in honesty. But she did.

Well, it was a fine pickle she found herself in. She didn't see any future for her and Elijah. He was a man who lived in a world completely different from her own, who lived by different standards than ruled her life.

It was ironic that another man had come into her life, wanting her simply because she was the daughter of David and Lisa McGee. The first time it had happened, she'd been devastated by what Bryan had done. He had wanted to marry her simply for her parents' fame, then go back to the jungle and make a name for himself. At least Elijah had been honest in his motives. Too bad his honesty didn't help ease the pain more.

Everything looked secure. Too bad it didn't help Elijah's fractured peace of mind. He felt like he was in quicksand. The harder he tried to get out, the further he sank.

Well, there was no alternative. He needed to go back to the room he shared with Abigail. He was ignoring his duty, and he'd never done that before. Stopping before the door, he lightly knocked. "It's me, Abigail," he whispered.

Nothing.

Fear pumped through his veins. He opened the door and found the room empty. Oh, no, had someone gotten to her? As he turned to race down the hall, Abigail stepped into the hall from the bathroom. A folded sheet was in her hands.

"What the hell were you doing?" A stupider question he hadn't uttered since he asked about the state of her virginity. He was batting a thousand today.

She didn't bother to answer that question. "Is everything okay?" she asked.

Nothing was okay, he wanted to shout. But most of his frustration had nothing to do with Abigail, and he couldn't take it out on her.

"Everything seems fine," he answered.

She walked past him into the room. She didn't meet his eyes.

"Why don't you get some sleep? Morning will be here too quickly."

She eyed him, then the bed.

"I'm going to sit here at the window and make sure everything is okay. You need the sleep more than I do."

She opened her mouth to protest, then shook her head. Stretching out on the bed, she turned away from him. He wanted to join her on that bed, no matter how many times he told himself he didn't. And that truth worried him.

When Elijah woke, the sky was still dark. He glanced at his watch. It was a little after six. He didn't think he would fall asleep, but apparently, his body knew better than he that it needed rest.

He had tried to read the documents last night with

the light from the street, but it had been next to impossible. He'd wanted to turn on the overhead light, but he didn't want to wake Abigail and face her, in addition to reading about Neil. There was only so much trauma a person could endure at one sitting without losing himself. And he knew he'd reached his limit.

Looking up, he saw Abigail stir on the bed. He was tempted to walk to the bed and finish waking her with a kiss. The strength of the temptation shocked him.

He glanced out the window again at the light, bathing the morning in its glow. It still was disorientating not experiencing a sunrise. He could well understand Abigail's fascination with it. He wouldn't mind sharing several more sunrises with her.

He halted his mind from wandering in that direction. Last night had to be an aberration, born out of his need and hurt. He had to do his job, and not spend time spinning his wheels thinking about sex.

He could use a cup of that coffee Abigail so loved.

He heard a noise from the bed. When he looked, Abigail was staring at him. There was a tinge of apprehension in her gaze.

"Good morning," he greeted her, mustering as much normalcy as he could when all he wanted to do was shuck his clothes and climb back into bed with her.

"Morning."

"I'm sorry I don't have any coffee for you this morning, but I thought we could grab a bite to eat before we went to the hospital."

"Sounds good. Give me a moment in the bathroom, then I'll join you."

He gathered his backpack and the briefcase. "I'll wait for you downstairs."

She smiled. "I won't be long."

Good for her word, she appeared downstairs eight minutes later. She'd braided her hair, and she held her hat in one hand, her backpack in the other.

"I'm impressed," he said as he stood.

"Why?"

"Because you said you wouldn't be long and you weren't. My experience with females has been when they say they won't be long, that means whenever they get done, they'll be down."

She eyed him. "And how vast is your experience with females?"

From her tone, he knew he'd asked for trouble. "I've worked with enough females to know that they sometimes don't speak the same language as men."

She stopped. "Elijah, I haven't had my coffee yet this morning. I'm not up to verbally fencing with you. Give me an hour, then I'll be up to sparring speed."

"Don't kid yourself, Abigail. You are always up to a good fight, no matter what."

From her glare, she obviously didn't appreciate his comment. She didn't say anything to him until they were at the restaurant and she had her second cup of coffee. Then she placed the cup on the table and pushed away her plate.

"What are your plans for today?" she asked him. From her manner, she appeared nervous. Hell, he was jumpy, too, not knowing how to act around her.

Just ignore what happened last night, a voice in his head whispered. It wasn't a good solution to the problem, but it was the only one he could come up with.

"First I wanted to check on both Jerry and the pilot before we plan anything."

Nodding, she followed him out of the restaurant, across the street to the hospital. There was a new set of nurses on duty. As they approached Jerry's room, they noticed an unusual amount of activity going in and out. Before they could ask anyone what was happening, a covered body was wheeled out into the hallway. The sheet slipped from the patient's face and they saw Jerry's still features.

Abigail turned to one of the nurses and asked what had happened. As the nurse tried to explain, Abigail held up her hand, slowing the woman down.

"What did she say?" Elijah asked. He had understood only a couple of words.

"They don't know. Apparently he was doing well last night when the duty nurse made her rounds. They don't have an explanation as to what caused his death."

A deep sense of loss rose up in him, but he fought the emotion. His gut feeling told him something was wrong and there was no time for grief. "How's the pilot?"

Abigail asked the nurse. "It appears he's okay."

"So it was just Jerry who mysteriously died."

He could tell from her expression that she was uneasy, too. "Yes."

As they started to walk away, the nurse called to them. Abigail went back and took the note the woman held out to her.

"What is it?" He pointed to the note.

Her fingers shook as she opened the piece of paper. It was in Spanish. Abigail noticed a name, Dave, their pilot from yesterday, and a number. "It appears Dave wants you to call him."

The certainty that something was wrong increased a hundredfold. Immediately, he located a phone and called the number on the note. On the first ring, the phone was answered.

"Dave, this is Elijah. What's wrong?"

"Get the hell out of that city."

"Why?"

"I have a local girl answering the phone for me. I actually have paying clients whom I service. Yesterday an American called and asked for me. Nesta didn't want me to lose the business and told the person I was flying an injured friend from the jungle to Cuidad Bolívar. The man said he'd call back. I think you've been made, Elijah."

Elijah cursed. "Thanks, Dave."

"Do you need a ride to somewhere, let's say in the States?"

They were definitely going to need help. The question was, how far did the double agents in the agency go? Was Neil the only person involved? Elijah didn't want to trust anyone, but he needed to get back to the States to put a plan into action. "Yeah, we could use a ride."

"There's a small airport on the west edge of the city," Dave said. "It will take me about forty-five minutes to get there."

"We'll be there." When he hung up the phone, Elijah faced Abigail.

Awareness that something was wrong was mirrored in her eyes.

"We need to get out of here. And fast."

He looked around and saw a man by the elevator,

watching them. Elijah pocketed the note, took Abigail's arm in his and began to lead her to the stairwell.

She glanced over her shoulder and saw the man following them. She needed no other explanation and picked up her stride to keep pace with Elijah.

He pushed open the door to the stairs and dragged her onto the landing. "Go down a flight."

There was a question in her eyes, but she turned and followed his directions. He waited behind the door. When it opened and the man following them emerged, Elijah stepped behind him and administered a sharp chop to the man's carotid artery. The man fell forward on the landing. Elijah had to fight the urge to pull out the man's identification. He knew in his gut who'd sent the guy. Abigail's face came into view as she ascended the stairs from below.

"Let's hurry." Elijah took the man's gun, hopped over the body and joined her.

Because of the tight space, Elijah didn't see the man behind Abigail until he got to the landing. She stood stiffly, watching Elijah.

The man raised his gun high enough that Elijah could see that he was pointing the muzzle at Abigail's back. He muttered a command.

"Elijah doesn't speak Spanish," Abigail hastily explained. "I'll need to translate your orders for him."

He nodded.

"Elijah, this man wants your gun," Abigail said, relating the gunman's command.

Elijah thought about the chances of disarming the man, but he realized that Abigail would surely pay for any mistake he made. A moan from the man on the landing above them filled the stairwell.

The second gunman purposely put the muzzle of

his gun at the base of Abigail's neck. Elijah didn't need any further encouragement to surrender his weapons. With care, he handed both guns to the stranger.

"Juan, get up," the second gunman growled in Spanish.

Juan murmured a profanity. He staggered to his feet and stumbled down the flight of steps to where Elijah stood. His partner handed him his gun.

The second gunman commanded them to move. It was obvious from his actions and tone he was wanting them to walk down the stairs to street level. Elijah didn't move, pretending he didn't understand.

The gunman glared at Elijah, then told Abigail to translate.

"This gentleman wants us to walk down the steps to a waiting car."

Elijah shot the gunman a venomous look. "Okay. I'll follow you."

He looked at Abigail, trying to warn her that she needed to be ready for anything he would do. Abigail gave him a small nod.

The second gunman followed closely behind Abigail, and Elijah and the first gunman followed behind them. Abigail had opened the door into the corridor when Elijah saw his chance. He kicked out and caught the man in front of him on his knee, causing it to buckle, and he tumbled into the door.

The man behind Elijah hesitated, giving him enough time to ram his elbow in the gunman's stomach. The air whooshed out of his lungs. While he doubled over, trying to catch his breath, Elijah hit him again on the back of his neck. The man crumpled like a cardboard box.

Elijah turned and lunged at the first man, catching him on the chin, knocking him out. Retrieving his gun, Elijah opened the door.

Abigail stood there, her face tight with worry.

"C'mon, let's get out of here while we've got the opportunity."

She glanced around him, looking at the exit door as if waiting for it to burst open.

Grabbing her arm, Elijah pushed her through the main lobby. "Don't worry, those two are sidelined for a while."

"I don't believe I much care for your job, Elijah," she gasped as they raced across the room.

He laughed. "I'll let you in on a little secret. I don't think I could do your job. Hospitals make me nervous." They had ever since his father's death.

She shook her head. "I find it hard to believe that anything could set you off your stride," she replied as he pushed open the front door.

She didn't know the half of it, he thought.

Chapter 9

Outside the hospital's main door, Elijah flagged down a cab. "There's an airport on the west edge of the city where we're going to meet Dave, the pilot from yesterday. Can you make the cabbie understand that?" Elijah asked Abigail.

"Yes, I think so." She explained his directions to the cabbie.

The man nodded.

"Were those guys yours?" she whispered. "I mean, did they work for the CIA?"

"I can't be sure," he hedged.

"Give it an educated guess."

"They worked for someone who knew about us. Dave got a call yesterday from an American."

"What—"

Elijah pointed to the taxi driver, who was looking at them in the rearview mirror. "Why don't we finish this conversation in a better place?"

Her gaze, unwavering and direct, met his. Whatever reassurance she needed, she seemed to get, because she nodded. "All right, but I'll make you keep your word." There was a steely tone in her voice, and he knew he was going to have to explain even more than he already had.

"Of that, I don't doubt." And you probably won't like what I have to say, he thought to himself.

She nodded and looked out at the traffic. Her chin jutted out in a stubborn angle that gave him a moment of amusement. He'd bet that Abigail was a handful when she was mad. It was an interesting thought.

"You've been mighty helpful, Abigail. How many languages do you know?"

"Six. Besides the Indian dialect, I know Portuguese, Spanish, French, Italian and English."

"So I could take you to France with me?"

"For what?" The minute the words were out of her mouth, she blushed.

His brow arched. "As an interpreter...and other things."

The stain on her cheeks spread down her neck. He had the urge to kiss the pulse beating below her ear.

Elijah shook off the hypnotic effect of her closeness. Last night he had been able to temporarily escape their room, needing the time away from Abigail to sort out the confusing tangle of emotions that she evoked in him. But today, there was nowhere for him to go.

To make sure they weren't being followed, he frequently looked over his shoulder out the rear window as the cabbie wove through the thick traffic of the town.

Finally, they turned down a two-lane road that led

to the airport. It wasn't a big facility. One local airline had a counter, and the other counter was for private bookings. After paying the cabbie in Venezuelan centimos, which he had obtained last night when he'd left Abigail alone, Elijah peeked into the interior of the building and didn't see Dave.

"Let's wait by the runway," Elijah said, joining her by their backpacks.

They picked up their few items and walked to a hangar on the runway.

Setting down her backpack, Abigail faced him. "All right. Now that we're alone, why don't you confirm what I already have suspicions about."

Abigail was certainly not one to beat around the bush. She came straight to the heart of a matter. He found her honest approach refreshing after having to deal with people who shaded their words with numerous meanings. Unrealistic in his job, but refreshing. It was a quality in her that he respected, and it drew him to her. His mind started to wander to what had happened between them last night. He remembered the taste of her lips, her satiny skin, the feeling of sinking—

He halted his wayward thoughts before they could go any further. This wasn't the time for erotic fantasies, no matter how pleasant.

"Jerry was murdered. I can't say how it was done, but there's a thousand different ways to kill someone who's lying helpless in bed," he replied, forcing his mind onto what they were discussing.

She paled.

It was hard for him to witness the fear in her eyes, but she needed to know what they were facing.

"Yesterday someone speaking English called

Dave's service, on the pretense of hiring him. The
secretary told the client that Dave was out flying an
injured friend to the hospital. Dave thinks we've been
made. After what happened in the hospital, so do I.''
He rubbed the back of his neck. "That's why we're
taking Dave up on his offer. The longer we stay here,
the greater our chances of running into someone else
who's going to try to get this briefcase from us and
do to us what they did to Jerry. Our mole's explanation will hold together much better if all who know
the truth are dead. I'm going to be made the bad guy
in this scenario.''

"And I will simply be a loose end that has to be
eliminated.''

He couldn't look her in the eye. It was good she
realized what trouble they were facing, but somehow
he couldn't take comfort in that fact. He was the one
who had dragged her into this mess. And it was up
to him to get her out. "Yes.''

She swallowed hard. "What are we going to do?''
There was a quiet confidence in her eyes that he
would have the answer. Oddly enough, her trust in
him humbled him. Others he'd worked with knew he
had a reputation of getting things done, but that was
from experience. Abigail's trust came from…what?

He didn't have an answer to that. Nor did he have
an answer to what they were going to do. He needed
to get to Terrence. And he was going to have to make
a copy of the papers he carried and find someplace
safe to stash them.

Abigail was still gazing at him as if he had answers
to all her questions.

"We're going to have Dave fly us out of here into
the States.''

"And then?" she pressed.

"We're going to take one step at a time, Abigail."

"In other words, you don't have a clue." Her gaze pinned him.

"You're wrong. I plan to contact Neil's boss and let him know what's going on. Once I talk to him, turn over the proof, we'll be in the clear."

"And we pray that we get to this man before Neil, is that it?"

"Not necessarily. Our information will hold up, no matter what Neil says."

"Oh, that will be a comforting thing to put on my tombstone. Her information cleared her. She was innocent. Dead, but innocent."

"Damn—"

"I'm right, aren't I, Elijah? What we do is pray we get to your boss before Neil gets to *us?*" She took a step toward him.

He started to reach for her, but at the last second, ran his fingers through his hair. "Yes, damn you, you're right." He knew he was acting like a jerk. It didn't matter that she'd hit the nail on the head, verbalizing the very fear flowing through his veins. He took a deep breath. "I'm sorry, Abigail. We're in a fix, and I won't lie to you about it."

She reached out and took his hand. "All I ask, Elijah, is that you tell me the truth. I can deal better with that than imagining things. You see, my imagination is very vivid and very active." Her eyes pleaded with him to understand. "It was a curse when I was a child and a challenge for my parents."

She wasn't the only one with a vivid imagination. "I'll try."

"Thank you."

They heard the airplane on its approach. By the time the old DC3 had landed and rolled to a stop, they were heading toward the plane. Dave appeared in the doorway.

"It's good to see you two. Have any trouble?" he asked as he took Abigail's backpack.

Elijah's dark look answered him.

"That bad, huh?" Dave helped Abigail up the stairs. "What happened?"

"We ran into some gentlemen at the hospital who were anxious to detain us. Permanently," Elijah explained as he sat down in the co-pilot's seat. "I stopped them temporarily."

"So my warning didn't come a moment too soon."

"I owe you," Elijah replied.

Dave sat in the pilot's seat and started the engines. "Where do you want to go?"

"Do you have enough fuel to get us to Houston?"

Dave studied Elijah for a moment, then nodded, avoiding any other questions. "Yup. The plane's gassed up and ready to fly. I figured that you might want to go somewhere in the States."

"If it's no problem, then, take us to Texas."

"What happened?" Neil asked. He leaned forward and readjusted the phone.

"They escaped."

He wanted to curse. Instead, he gritted his teeth, trying to hold his temper in check. "Did you at least carry out the job I asked you to do?"

"I got that done. That guy won't be doing any talking."

Somehow the reassurance didn't help. "Are there any signs of them?"

"No."

"Have you checked the airport and the train station?"

"Not yet."

"Then, I'd say you have a lot more work to do before you next contact me. And I want answers, not guesses. Do you understand?"

"Yes."

He hung up the phone and sighed. Of all the people to be pitted against, Elijah Kendrick was the most determined and thorough. He knew, because he'd taught Elijah himself. And of all the people he had to deceive, why did it have to be Elijah?

Neil cursed again.

Elijah sat in the co-pilot's chair and read through the damning documents that Jerry had gotten from the East German. It made him sick to see the price Neil had gotten for each person he'd turned over. The price was doubled and tripled when Neil supplied the name of the control office who recruited the spy. Meeting places and information was included.

"Damn," Elijah muttered to himself.

He was surprised that the East Germans had let as much information out as they had. But he knew they also supplied a lot of bogus information through their double agents, designed to throw the CIA off.

Elijah had known half of the agents that had been given up. And he saw the faces of the deceased.

One name in particular brought back vivid memories. It had been 1985, during Elijah's first venture in East Germany. He was trying to buy information on the shipment of some nukes to China and had convinced a man who worked at the arms factory to sell the information. But the man never showed up for their meeting. Elijah had gone to the man's apartment and found his body—he'd been shot in the head. There'd been no note to indicate that he'd killed himself and no evidence of the papers he'd claimed he could get.

That man's death had haunted Elijah. Was it something *he'd* done? Was he somehow responsible for what happened?

As it turned out, the problem hadn't been with Elijah but with the person to whom he'd reported. It turned his stomach to see what Neil had done.

Neil's code name, Trojan Horse, was used throughout the East German documents. The last sheet, with Neil's name handwritten in the corner, was labeled Trojan Horse and described how he'd been recruited and gave a tally of monies paid to him over the years.

Elijah closed the file and slipped it back into the briefcase. His gaze met Abigail's. She offered no words of comfort or excuses, but she silently told him that he was not alone.

It didn't lessen the pain, but her comfort helped him endure.

After what he'd just read, he made himself a promise. Neil would pay.

They landed at Houston's Hobby Field in the early afternoon.

"If you need anything, let me know, Dave." Elijah held out his hand and waited for the other man to shake it.

"Don't worry about it."

"I won't forget." There was steel in Elijah's voice. Taking Abigail's arm, Elijah helped her down the steps into the hot, moist air of the October day. Houston might never get extremely cold, but it was always humid. They walked across the runway and entered the terminal then stopped at the security checkpoint, where Elijah showed his gun and badge to the official. Once they were on the concourse, Elijah pulled out his wallet and handed Abigail a ten. "I'm thirsty. Would you get me something to drink?"

"Are you really thirsty or do you just want me to get lost for a few minutes?"

The corner of his mouth kicked up. He was learning quickly that he wasn't able to slip things by Abigail. "Both."

She took the money and headed toward the restaurant at the end of the concourse.

He turned to the phones, dialed the main CIA number in Langley, Virginia, and asked for assistant secretary Terrence Roades.

After a moment, Terrence Roades's secretary came on the line. "Mr. Roades is on vacation for the next few days. Mr. Teatly is handling all his calls. Would you like to speak to him?"

Wouldn't that be dandy, speaking to Neil? he thought sourly. *Hey, Neil, I know you're the scumbag who's been selling out our agents around the globe. Tell me, does money ease your conscience when you lay your head on the pillow? Is it a warm mistress on a cold night? Can you shave in the morning without wanting to slit your own throat? How could you betray friends?*

"Sir?" the secretary asked again.

He hung up without answering her. He frowned at the phone as if it was the equipment's fault that Terrence wasn't there.

Vacation? What the hell was Terrence doing? He knew about the East German agent and knew they had sent Jerry after the papers. Elijah rubbed the back of his neck. What was going on?

He tried to think back to remember if he'd seen Terrence before he left. No, he couldn't recall seeing him that last day in Langley. He'd seen Neil, had talked with him about the buy in Buenos Aires. Neil had seemed anxious and determined to find Jerry and learn the identity of the mole....

Elijah shook his head, shaking off the past. He had to concentrate on the here and now. What was he going to do?

If Terrence was actually on vacation, he would have taken his cell phone with him. Elijah smiled, then carefully went through his memory for the number. After a moment, he recalled it and dialed.

After several rings, the operator's voice came on the line and said, "The customer is unavailable."

He hung up the phone and frowned. It was unusual that he couldn't get through. Something had to be wrong. Of course, Terrence's twins were both pre-schoolers and maybe they had done something to the phone. Now what?

He was sure Neil had already blackened his name within the agency, and if he called again, he risked the caller ID showing were he was located. If he was arrested and his papers seized, then he'd really be in a world of hurt.

What he needed to do was make a copy of the papers and hide them with someone he trusted. Jon Michaels immediately popped into his brain. If something happened to him, Jon would bring Neil down.

But beyond copying the papers, Elijah needed to

find Terrence. He would verify Elijah's innocence and his involvement in the mission. And only Terrence could guarantee Abigail's safety.

Elijah walked away from the phones and went into the little kiosk where Abigail was sitting at a table, devouring an ice cream cone.

"I was hungry," she explained. "I don't travel well on an empty stomach." She nodded toward the cup on the table. "That's tea for you."

He sat down. He grasped the paper cup and absently took a drink, his mind concentrating on the problems at hand. What should they do now? he wondered, scowling. Where had Terrence gone? Was he really on vacation?

"Elijah, is everything all right?" Abigail asked, wiping off her hands with a napkin.

"We've run into a little problem."

"So what else is new?" she shot back. A flush stained her cheeks.

Silently, he agreed with her. Nothing, absolutely nothing had gone right since he learned that the plane had gone down. A bark of laughter escaped his lips.

She stared at him as if he'd lost what little common sense he had.

"It's either laugh or let out a string of oaths that would singe your ears." And would accurately reflect his frustrations.

That brought a frown to her lovely face. "What was the bad news this time?"

Her voice brought him out of his mental wandering. "The guy I needed to contact at the agency is supposedly on vacation."

Her face paled. "Vacation?"

"It doesn't make sense, does it?"

She looked around, as if trying to take in the enormity of what they were facing. "No. Did he know about the downed plane?"

"Yes. That's why things don't add up."

"Where would he go?"

Elijah started to shake his head, when an idea sparked in his mind. "Terrence has a cabin in the Sangre de Cristo Mountains of northern New Mexico, close to Santa Fe. He and his wife have spent the last couple of years fixing it up after the birth of their kids."

"Do you think he's there?"

"At this point, it can't hurt to look. Terrence and his wife love hiking. I've been to their cabin several times, so I know where it is."

"Why not just call them?" she asked.

"There's not a phone in the cabin. Terrence brings his cell phone with him. I tried that number already, but it's not working at the moment."

As soon as they finished eating, they went to the Southwest Airlines gate that announced a flight to Albuquerque. They did not go into the lobby of the airport, therefore Elijah didn't have to show security his gun.

"Do you fly to Santa Fe?" Elijah asked the woman behind the counter.

"No, but we do fly into Albuquerque. Would that be acceptable?"

It was a short drive between the cities. He looked at the time of departure. The next flight was to leave in twenty minutes. The one after that, in three hours. He wouldn't have time to copy the papers he carried, even if there was someplace in the airport to make copies, and still make the next plane. He would copy them when they arrived in Albuquerque and send them to Jon.

"Sure, that's okay." Pulling out his wallet, he said, "I'd like two tickets on that flight."

The woman behind the counter issued the tickets and handed them to him, then took up the handheld microphone and announced the flight would begin to board.

He turned to Abigail. "You ready?"

She nodded and followed him down the jetway to the plane.

Elijah pulled out the airline magazine in the pocket of the seat before them and began to scan it. It was obvious to Abigail that he wasn't going to talk.

"Elijah…" Abigail began.

He rested the magazine on his lap, waiting for her to continue. She could tell from his body language that he was preparing himself for her questions.

"Why did you stop and talk to the captain?"

He leaned over and whispered, "I've got my gun, Abigail. Police officials are supposed to declare their weapons to the pilot. I told him who I was and that I had my gun. It prevents trouble down the line, and I think we've had our share, don't you?"

She didn't look comforted. "Won't he report it?"

"I doubt it. They're used to the FBI and other police agencies traveling with their weapons."

"Oh." She bit her lip, then asked, "Can't you tell me anything more about what happened when you phoned the agency?" A couple of times since they boarded the flight, Abigail had tried to question him, but he gave her a look that told her this was not the time. Well, they'd been on this flight for nearly an hour, and she didn't care to finish the last forty minutes of the flight with her own demons chasing around her brain.

He glanced around, making sure no one else was listening or interested in them. "As you know, the man I wanted to talk to was on vacation. The person filling in for him was the very individual who is the source of the problem."

Her fingers tightened around the plastic cup that contained the last of her soda.. "So, you're in trouble."

He leaned close and whispered in her ear, "Not me, Abby. We."

Her gaze flew to his. Although there was a cautious note in his eyes, that caution turned to heat as he stared at her lips. She felt the caress as strongly as if he'd actually kissed her. Her tongue darted out to moisten her dry lips. His eyes narrowed.

"You're playing with fire, Abby," he warned her in a low voice.

She gulped the last of her drink and glanced out the window. She'd been desperately trying to forget what had happened between them the previous night, but it was impossible. Each moment was burned into her brain. As she sat next to Elijah, his big six-foot-four frame blotted out her awareness of all the other individuals on the plane. All she could think about was how his fingers had felt on her skin, the wonder of his lips, the waves of hunger followed by the ultimate release into the heavens.

She reminded herself that Elijah was only beside her now because he had to be. Last night had been an aberration. He had needed her, needed the warmth of her touch, the reassurance that he wasn't alone. But that magical time might not translate into something that would last for more than a few hours. It certainly hadn't lasted long after they'd made love. Elijah had jumped back like a scalded cat.

Now he lightly brushed his fingers over her jaw. She turned to him as he asked, "It's my guess you want to know what we're going to do if Terrence isn't at the cabin?"

Her skin still tingled where he touched her. "That only makes sense."

"Right now, I'm praying—"

Her brow went up at his use of the word *prayer.*

He noted her shock. Clearing his throat, he continued, "I'm praying that Terrence is in New Mexico. If he isn't, I'll need some time to think, to come up with an alternative plan and figure out what's really going on." He picked up her hand and held it in his own. "It's like my legs have been shot out from beneath me, and I have to learn to walk again."

"Are you close to this individual?"

His mouth tightened and his eyes grew distant. "I thought I was. To be betrayed by an enemy is understandable. But by a friend is..."

He closed his eyes, and his hand tightened around hers. She felt helpless in the wake of the pain radiating from him. She wanted somehow to comfort him. Unable to stop herself, she pulled his hand up to her lips and kissed it. When she looked at him again, his gaze was fixed on her, as if to try to decipher the motive behind her actions.

"How are we going to get to this cabin?" she asked, desperate to divert her mind from the feeling of his warm palm. All she could concentrate on was his skin touching hers and how it had felt to have those hands roaming over her body.

She shook her head, trying to clear it of those heated thoughts. Why was she so vulnerable to this man's touch? Why did her mind seem to disconnect from her body when he was near?

His fingers tightened around hers. "Drive. The cabin is in the mountains just north of Santa Fe."

"Oh." Then, after a moment, she asked, "Have you ever brought another female there?" The instant the question was out of her mouth, Abigail wanted to take it back. She was shocked at her jealousy. The question had just tumbled out of her mouth without conscious thought. It was none of her business whom Elijah associated with. And although they were technically married, it wasn't the real thing, with them both resolving to be devoted to each other.

His brow arched. "Are you jealous?"

"I'm sorry, Elijah. I don't know what came over me." She shrugged. "I think I've had enough surprises on this trip to last me a lifetime."

They'd trooped through the jungle, gotten married and been chased by murderers.

"I can second that," Elijah said. "I do have another friend," he continued, "who lives out in this area of the country." His voice was light, and she knew he was trying to get a reaction out of her.

"Are you going to tell me who this friend is?"

"*He's* a friend I met in college." There was an indulgent quality to his voice. "The last two years I was in college, I went home with Ted on holidays."

"What about your sister?"

"She was with her adoptive family."

His tone was cold, not inviting her to question him

further, but she'd never been good about heeding warnings. "What do you mean?"

He rolled his head on the seat, and his fingers brushed back several strands of her hair that had worked loose from her braid. For a moment, he seemed lost in the feel of her hair. When his heated gaze met hers again, she knew he'd been reliving last night. Finally, he pulled his hand back and sighed.

"After my dad died, my sister and I were separated. But she was lucky and found a permanent family to adopt her. I was raised in a series of foster homes. No one wanted a sullen, skinny kid who was looking for trouble."

There was a wealth of unspoken hurt in his words, which touched her. He was a man who never felt like he belonged. Never had a place that was his own. Never had parents who could ease the troubled dreams of the night. And never thought he needed anyone.

But she got the feeling that their lovemaking last night had taken him as much by surprise as it had her. She couldn't deny that from the moment they'd met an awareness had hummed between them, and they had tried to ignore it.

Last night, she couldn't have turned away from Elijah no matter what the consequences. The betrayals he had experienced in his life had struck close to his heart. And it had been there in his eyes, in the need of his lips, and in the desperation of his touch.

But in struggling to bury the hurt, they had both uncovered something else. In coming together, they had bonded. Touched a part of each other no other had.

She felt bound to him. She didn't know if Elijah

felt the same way, but at this point, it was simply borrowing trouble to guess at tomorrow.

"What about your parents, Abigail?"

His question drew her out of her thoughts. "You know about my parents. They worked among the Indians, putting down their native language into written form, then taught them to read and write that language."

"What were your parents like?"

He was wanting something from her, but she couldn't imagine what it was. "They were incredibly patient not only in their work, but with me and my sister. I wasn't exactly what you would call a model child."

A laugh escaped his lips. She stared at him in stunned amazement.

"Now, why don't I find that hard to believe? You wouldn't want to tell me—"

"No." She flushed to the roots of her hair.

He shrugged.

"I think I've been very cooperative given the circumstances," she defended herself. "It's your actions that have been..."

"Yes?" He waited for her to finish.

She looked out the window of the plane. "Don't you tire of the lies and deception? Doesn't it dry up your soul not to be able to believe in another man's word?"

"Wake up, Abigail. The world operates on the premise that you get what you can while you can. And people will do anything to get it."

Her gaze didn't waver from his. "No, Elijah, not everyone in this world functions on that assumption.

The people I work with on that mountain in Kentucky don't operate with those rules.''

He closed his eyes and rested his head on the seat. ''Sounds like heaven.'' He touched her hand. ''Too bad the rest of the world isn't like that.''

Elijah was hoping that an alternative plan of action, as to what they should do if they didn't find Terrence at his cabin, would occur to him on the flight from Houston to Albuquerque. The fact that Terrence was unavailable bothered him. That meant something big was going down. And usually if someone as high up in the agency as Terrence was out of touch, that meant the White House was involved.

But as he thought about backup plans, glimpses of the previous night with Abigail popped into his head. Each time he let down his guard, there they were, visions of delight, tastes of heaven. And each time he realized what he was doing, he cracked down on the thoughts, pushing them to the back of his mind, where they lurked.

And when he wasn't battling his own body's reactions to his memories, there was Abigail, leaning close to him, filling his vision with her beauty, filling his nostrils with the delicate fragrance that was her own. So not only did he have his own body to wrestle with, he had to fight against the lure of hers. He wasn't winning any battles.

What if Terrence wasn't at his cabin? What would they do then? He didn't know, but maybe there, with a little more room between him and Abigail, his head would get clearer and he'd be able to think.

Yeah, right, he grumbled to himself. And when had he taken up the art of self-delusion?

Since he met Abigail McGee.

He cursed and looked out the window. Forcing his mind away from Abigail, he thought about the problems facing them in Albuquerque.

They needed money. Untraceable money, so he couldn't tap into his bank account, nor could he allow Abigail to use any of her credit cards. The money he'd brought along with him was almost gone. He hadn't planned on running from his own guys, not for this long, anyway.

Who could he call for help? Did he want to gamble on someone in the Company? What if Neil had accomplices? Or even if Neil was alone in his actions, a misplaced word from an individual to Neil could indicate where he and Abigail were hiding.

He was tempted to call his sister. May had married several years ago and was raising a family in a suburb of Tulsa. He could call her and get the cash, but he couldn't be sure that her phone wouldn't be tapped. Neil was sharp enough to cast his net around a suspect's family until they showed up.

Jon's name popped into his brain again. For two years he'd hidden Jon and watched out for Jon's wife. But would Neil remember that he had been Jon's contact man? Neil had been in Russia during that time, and Jon had left the Company soon after, so chances were good that Neil hadn't heard of him. As soon as they landed, he would call Jon and warn him about the situation. And get funds from him.

Yeah, Jon would help. He could even help with finding Terrence. Jon still had contacts. And Elijah knew he and Abby needed all the help they could get.

Chapter 10

"We will be landing in Albuquerque in five minutes," the flight attendant's voice announced over the intercom. "Please hand the cabin crew any trash you have."

The announcement brought Elijah out of his thoughts.

"You were concentrating mighty hard," Abigail commented.

"Just daydreaming."

Her disbelief was clearly reflected in her deep blue eyes. "Oh, please, Elijah. You, of all men, are not given to flights of fancy. Everything that goes on in your brain has a definite purpose."

She knew him too well. He had stopped daydreaming the day his father had died. From then on, he'd only thought of things he could do, things he could control, not on how things should be. He'd been on the short end of the stick too many times. He knew if he wanted to have the better end of a deal, he had to plan it.

"So what were you thinking about?" she asked again.

"I was wondering how we were going to get some money to buy food and gas to drive to my friend's cabin."

Her fingers came up and touched the gold-and-diamond necklace that hung around her neck. He clearly remembered tracing that chain with his tongue the night before. Quickly, he shut down those thoughts. "How much money do you have left?"

She looked through her backpack and found her wallet. There was a five there. She handed it to him.

"With the little I have left, that gives us a grand total of fifteen dollars."

"We could pawn my necklace. It should bring enough for us to pay for a car rental and some groceries."

"If we need to. I'll be sure to keep your offer in mind."

As they deplaned and walked into the terminal, Elijah knew that he was going to have to use his emergency credit card and ID to get them the car. He stopped and pulled Abigail aside.

"In order for us to rent a car, I'm going to have to leave a credit card imprint. And to verify the credit card, I'll have to give the auto company my driver's license number."

"I assume you're telling me this because what you're going to do might take me by surprise if I wasn't warned?"

"Ah, Abigail, you're a girl after my own heart."

She didn't respond.

"I wanted to warn you before we got to the rental agency."

"Who are you going to be?"

"Jack Williams."

As it turned out, the woman at the desk was charmed by Elijah. She gave only a cursory look at his driver's license, which was registered in North Carolina.

"How do you like North Carolina?" she asked as she wrote down his driver's license number.

"I love it."

"My sister lives in Durham. She loves it there."

"I drive through Durham every day to go to work. It's a wonderful place."

She smiled at him and pointed him to where they could pick up the car.

Once they were in the car, Abigail stared in amazement at Elijah. "I don't believe you were that calm. My stomach was doing back flips."

"It comes with practice, Abigail. When your life depends on being something you're not, you become an excellent actor."

With his words ringing in her ears, she wondered if his acting ability had covered what happened last night.

"Can we use that bogus credit card of yours for other expenses?" Abigail asked Elijah as they pulled out of the airport parking lot.

"No. We use different identities against the bad guys, but those precautions don't protect us from inside betrayal. Neil knows I have an emergency identity and credit cards and he knows me well enough that he'll probably be able to guess what name I have on them. I don't want to give us away to him."

"Why would he be able to guess that?"

"Jack is my father's name and Williams is my mother's maiden name. It wasn't very creative on my part, but then I never figured I'd be hiding from my own. I'll know better next time." His voice was hard. He wouldn't make that same mistake twice. "The car company won't turn in the actual bill until I return the car, then I'll pay in cash. The receipt will be destroyed, so essentially, no one will see it. It won't go on a record where Neil could look. We'll still be in the clear."

"So what you're telling me is we still need money," she said.

Poor Abigail. She was caught in his nightmare. He wanted to apologize, but there was nothing he could say that would change the situation.

"Afraid so. People don't question cash. But I'm going to call a friend and see if I can get money from him."

As he drove out of the airport, he kept scanning the area, looking for a copy place. He came across one in a strip shopping center. Pulling in, he grabbed the briefcase. "I'll be just a minute," he told Abigail as he opened his door.

She didn't seem inclined to follow him.

The place was empty, which was a relief. He made two copies of the document and bought two mailers from the cashier. "Where's the closest post office?"

The man pointed back the direction from where they'd come. "Back two blocks, then take a right. It's hard to miss."

Elijah picked up the marker on the counter. "Mind if I use this?"

"Help yourself."

Quickly Elijah addressed one of the envelopes to his apartment in Washington. The other he addressed to Jon in McKinney, Texas. "Thanks," Elijah said, nodding at the man. When he got back into the car, he handed Abigail the mailers and set the briefcase in the back seat.

"Why are you mailing this to yourself?" She looked up. "Oh...insurance?"

"It's an added precaution." He pulled out into traffic. "The clerk assured me that there's a post office down here a couple of blocks."

It was easy to find. The brand-new building stood out among the other older structures. Abigail went inside with him this time.

"How do you deal with this tension?" she quietly asked him as he waited in line.

He looked down into her large blue eyes. When he was working overseas, he'd enjoyed the thrill of the chase, being on edge all the time. But he could understand how off balance she felt.

"It's that extra shot of adrenaline that keeps you sharp. There are a million details that you have to keep track of, and if you don't—"

"May I help you?" the clerk asked.

They stepped up to the counter and Elijah used most of their remaining money to mail the envelopes. As they were leaving, Elijah saw a pay phone. He pulled Abigail across the lobby, stopped before it and made a collect call. By the fourth ring, the automatic answering service clicked on.

"Your party isn't there. Please try again," the operator informed him.

Elijah hung up. "Jon's not there."

"What would you do if you were out of the country?" she asked.

"I'd go to my dead drop." Seeing her frown, he added, "That's a place where your contact leaves money in case you have to get out of somewhere quickly."

"Is there someone else you trust?"

In light of Neil's betrayal, there was no one he was willing to gamble on. "I'll wait for Jon."

Her stomach growled. "I'm hungry now."

It had been more than ten hours since they'd had breakfast in Venezuela, and the ice cream she'd had at the airport wasn't much. Of course, there were the peanuts on the plane but that didn't begin to fill the hole she felt.

"I think we should pawn my necklace. Later we can come back and redeem it."

He didn't like the idea of doing that, but they needed cash to eat. He pulled out the phone directory and looked for the closest pawn shop.

"Why don't you get the map the rental company supplied and we'll check it against these addresses."

When she returned with the map, they discovered one of the shops was only a couple of blocks away.

As they pulled into Stanley's Pawn Shop's parking lot, Abigail bit her bottom lip. Elijah turned off the engine and sat back.

"Are you sure you want to do this?"

She couldn't maintain her composure, and glanced away. "Yes."

She reached around her neck and tried to release the catch. Her movements were clumsy as she fumbled with the delicate chain.

"Here, I'll do that." Brushing away her hands, Elijah took over the job of releasing the catch. Her skin was soft and smooth, making him want to stop and kiss her at the base of her neck.

She closed her eyes at his touch, which only made his job harder.

"There," he commented as the catch gave way. A shiver ran through her. He wanted to pull her against his chest and allow his lips to play with the tender skin. The feelings he hadn't dealt with this morning, but shoved aside, were cropping up with regular frequency and at the worst of times. Why couldn't he bring his desires into line? Why was he thinking about her when he ought to be thinking about saving their butts?

She held the necklace while he unclasped the ends of the chain. Looking down at the piece of jewelry, moisture gathered in her eyes.

His hand closed over hers as she held the necklace. "We don't have to do this, Abigail. I can come up with another way to get some money." He didn't know what, but he sure could try.

She tried to smile, but it was a poor imitation. "How? You going to rob a store? We could wait for your friend, but I want to eat now, not later. This is the best way."

He hesitated, then nodded and took the necklace from her. Coming around the car, he opened her door and waited for her.

"If it's just the same to you, I'll wait in the car."

He couldn't help but feel she had just given him something very precious. And if it was the last thing he did, he'd redeem it for her.

"When this is over, I'll come back and get this for you," he told her softly.

Abigail watched Elijah disappear into the pawn shop, her necklace in his hand. Her grandparents had given her the pendant on her fifteenth birthday. It had been her first birthday after her family had come back from the jungle. She had missed the friends she'd made in the tribe, and her parents and grandparents had tried to make that birthday extra special for her. Her sister had been presented with a similar necklace on her birthday the next month. Since that day, Abigail hadn't taken it off.

She wouldn't have believed she could part with it, but it wasn't as if she were selling it. They'd come back for it, she told herself.

Closing her eyes, Abigail rested her head on the seat. Her life had certainly been turned upside down in the last seventy-two hours.

Three days, is that all it had been?

Opening her eyes, she glanced at the adobe building in front of her. And what was she doing here? Running.

A police cruiser pulled into the parking space next to the car.

"Good afternoon," the officer said through her open window as he climbed out of his car.

Abigail forced herself to smile at the cop. "Morning."

At that instant Elijah exited the pawn shop. For a fraction of a second, he hesitated, then strode out to the car. He nodded to the policeman.

Elijah didn't say anything until they had pulled into the street. "Did the cop ask you anything?" He glanced into the rearview mirror to make sure no one was following them.

She thought that perhaps his reaction was a bit excessive, but what did she know about spying except what she saw on old reruns of "Mission Impossible"? "All he did was smile and say good afternoon." Her stomach growled again.

Elijah's eyebrows shot up. "I guess I'd better feed you, quickly."

He made it sound like it was her fault she hadn't eaten. "Aren't you hungry?"

His gaze didn't waver from the street. "I could use something to eat. You like Mexican?" he asked, pointing to the Casa Ole sign.

Briefly she wondered what he'd do if she said she didn't. "As long as it's food, I'll be happy." But her mouth was watering and she was ready to eat.

"Are you always this easy to please?" There was a tone in his voice that let her believe that his question referred to more than just food.

How could she answer that? "I'm a very genial person." She ignored his surprised expression.

"We should all be so easygoing," he mumbled.

"What's that crack supposed to mean?"

"I just wish all my operatives were as easy to please."

He pulled into the drive-through lane of the restaurant. "I'll order a couple of burritos and tacos. They have wonderful sopaipillas."

"How do you know?" she asked more in surprise than anything else.

"The last time I was in New Mexico, Terrence and his wife brought me to the Casa Ole in Santa Fe. It's the same style building, therefore I assume they're owned by the same people." He rolled down his window and placed the order.

"That will be ten fifteen," the voice in the drive-through replied.

He drove up to the window and paid the woman handling the orders.

As they waited for their food, he said, "I wish there had been another way, Abigail, besides hocking your necklace, but we're kinda behind the old eight ball."

There was a wealth of understanding in his eyes. Somehow, his knowing what her sacrifice had cost her made it easier. She didn't think she was one of those people who were transparent with their feelings. But apparently Elijah could read her as easily as a billboard on the freeway. The prospect was scary.

"What happens if your boss isn't at his cabin?" She wanted to move the conversation to a more neutral ground.

"Your order, sir," the woman in the window said.

"Thanks." Elijah took the sacks from her and looked at Abigail as he drove away. "We can look for a park or eat here in the parking lot. The choice is yours."

She laughed. "That is the first time since I've known you, Elijah, that you've given me a choice."

Amazingly enough, he blushed. "Then, take it and hurry."

"I think there was a park back a block. Why not eat there?"

"Okay, but we'll have to make it fast." He nodded and turned onto the street. Doubling back, he back-tracked to the park. There were swings and monkey bars. On the edge of the playground was a picnic table. They parked in the lot, then made their way to the table.

After they sat down and started on their burritos,

Abigail said, "You never answered my question, Elijah. And if I've learned anything about you, it's that you don't leave details like that to the last minute."

Surprise shone in his eyes. "Are you sure you wouldn't like to change careers? You're mighty good at reading me, and I've a reputation as being stone-faced and hard to read."

"I'm sure. Now, what if your boss isn't at his cabin?"

He popped the last bite of burrito into his mouth. "It means that Terrence didn't go on vacation. When I tried his cell phone, it wasn't working, either. I'll call again in a few minutes and check."

"So what does that mean?"

"It can mean several things. He could've been called to the White House and asked to go on some mission for them. It would be very hush-hush, and Terrence wouldn't communicate with anyone until he was done. There was a time last year when the Russians allowed him into their KGB files to check out certain rumors about MIAs from Vietnam. No one wanted to say anything until we knew the status of things."

"Oh."

He shrugged. "It could be any number of things. I'll get a newspaper and look through it. I might be able to glean something from it."

"Who is this person you mailed a copy of the papers to?" she asked.

"He was one of my agents who was stationed in London. Jon's retired now—as much as you can retire from the CIA—and living with his wife here in the States. They're in Texas right now. I've tried to come up with someone else active in the agency, but there's no one I trust more than Jon.'' There was a haunted look in his eyes.

''You trusted your boss, didn't you?''

''Yeah.''

That was all he said, but there was a world of hurt in his voice. And the starkness of his response reemphasized for her how deep the hurt went.

''If Terrence isn't at his cabin, Jon could call Langley and ask to speak to Terrence, and only him—on some urgent matter that only Terrence can deal with. If anyone can get information out of Terrence's secretary, it's Jon.''

''Okay.''

A mother and her preschool girl walked to the swings. The little girl smiled and waved at them. ''Look, Momma, they're having a picnic.''

Abigail waved back at the little girl. When she turned back to Elijah, she asked, ''Do you think that will work?''

''Let's tackle that problem when and if it arises. But getting to Terrence is the important thing. We'll show him our proof, and he'll be able to take out Neil.''

She paused. ''Is that going to work, Elijah? Didn't you say that your boss was going to put out the word that you're the corrupt one?''

''There's always a possibility that things won't go our way, but I think with Jon on our side, we'll have a fighting chance.''

''But you can't guarantee that.''

He sat back. ''In this life, only death and taxes are guaranteed.''

''You need to work on your bedside manner, Elijah. It stinks.''

"My job, Abigail, is not to provide comfort, but to keep this country safe."

They were not easy words to hear.

Before they left the city, they stopped by a grocery store. Elijah wanted to get in contact with Jon before they left for the mountains. There wasn't a phone in the cabin. With lines always going down, Terrence brought his cell phone with him when he was there.

"I need to make a call," Elijah told her as he climbed out of the car. He leaned down and said, "Why don't you go inside and purchase some necessities—sandwich makings, bread, lunch meats, tomatoes, coffee, tea and some fruit? It will help if Terrence isn't there, and if he is, we'll add to his stores."

She eyed him. It seemed that she read through his ruse to have her doing something while he tried again to get hold of Jon.

"Okay." She slid out of the car and waited until he joined her. Holding out her hand, she said, "I'll need some money."

He handed her two twenties. "If you need more, I'll be right here."

At first she looked like she would protest, then she nodded. "Do you want me to make a loud quacking noise when I leave the store?" she asked in a deadpan tone.

A bark of laughter erupted from his throat. "I'll notice you. Don't worry."

There was a heated look in her eyes that found an answering response in him. She turned and entered the store. He turned to the phone and dialed Jon's number.

"Hello." A woman answered the phone. For an

instant, Elijah thought he had dialed the wrong number, because in the background there was a very unhappy baby.

"Lauren, where are you?" Jon's voice floated through the line. "We've got trouble."

Elijah knew he'd dialed the right number. "May I speak to Jon?" he asked.

It took a moment for Jon Michaels to get to the phone. "Yeah?" His frustration rang clearly in his voice.

"It appears I called at a bad moment," Elijah said.

Jon laughed. "I thought I was in trouble when I was hiding out in London after my partner's murder. Let's just say that time is mild compared to having to take care of an eighteen-month-old baby."

"My congratulations on your daughter."

There was a silence on Jon's side. "What's the matter, Elijah? You've already sent us best wishes on the birth of Caroline."

"Is your line secure?"

"Yes."

Elijah sighed. "The guy who betrayed you wasn't the only mole in the organization. Things have been going wrong for the last ten years. Somehow many of our top agents have been compromised. Well, I've finally been able to track down the traitor. It's Neil Teatly."

"Your boss?" There was a tone of amazement in Jon's voice, like he couldn't quite believe his ears. Elijah felt the same.

"The one and only." He explained about his trip to the Amazon. "When I called this afternoon, I discovered Neil's superior and the guy I need to go to, Terrence Roades, who I know is clean, is supposedly out on vacation. Conveniently, Neil is taking his calls.''

"Vacation?'' Disbelief rang in Jon's voice.

"My feelings exactly. Something's going on, and I don't know what it is.''

"Did you try Terrence's cell phone?''

"Yeah, and something's wrong with the unit. I need to find Terrence and take him the evidence. I'm taking a gamble he's at his mountain retreat north of Santa Fe. If that backfires, then I'm going to need your help, Jon. If I don't miss my guess, Neil will float the story that I'm the bad egg and will need to be stopped no matter what. So now, not only will I have to dodge the bad guys, but our guys, as well. I need you to discover if that has already happened.''

"You're hip deep in this mess, aren't you?''

"Not only me, Jon. There's a woman with me. She helped while we were in the jungle. She's been unwillingly dragged into it.''

"So what do you want me to do?'' Jon asked.

"You know Terrence's secretary, don't you?''

"Yeah, she was a big help with all the papers after I resigned.''

"Didn't you two date a couple of times?''

"What are you angling at, Elijah?''

"I think Sandra just might tell you where her boss is vacationing—if he's vacationing at the moment. Would you try and get that information for me?''

"I'm a married man, Elijah, and I take my vows seriously.'' There was a light note in Jon's voice.

"Don't give me that, Jon. I'm not asking for anything beyond a friendly phone call. Besides, I think turnaround is fair play.'' He was desperate and needed to press his advantage.

"You're going for the big guns, huh? You must feel your back is against the wall."

"I feel like I'm drowning."

"Do you have a number where I can reach you?" Jon asked.

"No. I'll call back tomorrow at twelve hundred hours. Will that give you enough time?"

"Should be. You need anything? You fixed for money and supplies?"

"Funny you should mention that. I'm going to need some cash."

"No problem. How much you going to need?"

"A couple of thousand should cover it."

"I'll wire it to you, just name the location."

Elijah looked around, then noticed the sticker in the grocery story window that stated they were a Western Union outlet. Elijah gave Jon the address of the store. "And by the way, you'll be receiving a package tomorrow. It's a copy of the papers I have. If anything happens to me, make sure Terrence sees them."

A baby's wail sounded in the background. "You take care, Elijah."

"Thanks." He replaced the handpiece in its cradle and took a deep breath. He felt better with Jon on their side. Someone was in the game now who knew who the players were and what their colors were. Maybe, just maybe, they might get out of this mess with their skins intact.

Elijah walked inside the store and began to look for Abigail, but his mind was filled with images of Jon. His friend's life had changed dramatically over the last two years. Elijah had been Jon's boss when Jon was acting as an agent in England. When Jon had gone back into the field after he recovered from a near-fatal accident, Elijah had watched with envy as Jon had again renewed his relationship with his wife. Elijah had felt a most unusual feeling—envy—when Jon quit his clandestine activities to devote his time to his wife and child.

Never having experienced that warm, safe haven of home and hearth, Elijah was skeptical that such a thing existed. But Jon had proved him wrong, and Elijah had felt guilty for feeling envious.

He spotted Abigail in the refrigerated section, picking up a dozen eggs. Oddly enough, he realized the envy that he'd felt for Jon was no longer there. Nor was the loneliness that had always haunted his soul. The realization of that truth hit him.

"Did you reach your friend?" she asked as she set the eggs in the basket.

"Yes. He's going to wire me money in the next few minutes."

"So we finally have someone in our corner." She smiled.

A answering grin curved his mouth. "And he's the best ally you'll ever have."

She stopped and stared at him. "You have a wonderful smile, Elijah. You should use it more."

He was captured by the look of wonder and longing in her eyes.

"Excuse me," a woman said, moving Abigail's cart so she could get to the eggs.

Abigail blushed and wheeled her cart away.

"Are you finished?" Elijah asked, walking behind her.

"Yes."

They walked in silence to the checkout counters.

"I'll wait over by the Western Union counter."

She nodded and got in line.

As he watched her, Elijah wondered what the hell was going on here. Why couldn't he keep his eyes on the goal—getting their butts out of this mess—instead of letting his mind wander onto the look in Abigail's eyes?

"Sir," the man at the Western Union counter called out. Elijah turned. "Your money's here."

He signed the receipt, then slipped the money into his wallet. He noticed the newspapers stacked by the window. If Terrence wasn't at his cabin, Elijah needed to try to figure out what had happened—why Terrence was unavailable. He bought a local paper, the *Washington Post,* and the *New York Times.* Thinking of Terrence, he walked outside and redialed the other man's cell phone number. The operator informed him the number still wasn't working.

As he hung up, Abigail exited the store.

"Are you finished?" she asked him.

"I've done as much as I can here. Let's go and see if I can find my boss."

"I hope our luck is changing."

"So do I," he grumbled.

Chapter 11

Elijah pulled out the map and checked the routes out of Albuquerque to Santa Fe. "We're going to be looking for Route 422 out of here, going to Santa Fe."

"All right."

He waited for Abigail to ask about the phone call. But she said nothing as he found the freeway and entered the flow of traffic. He could feel her waiting, her expectations. She had either gotten better at reining in her feelings or she was reading him better, because she was waiting for him to tell her what had happened.

"Jon, the ex-agent I told you about, the one who wired me the money, is going to try to discover where Terrence is vacationing if he isn't at his cabin. I'll call him back tomorrow at noon. And I got the money, so we're fixed that way."

He glanced at her. In the waning light of day, he could see the smile that curved her lips.

"Why the smile?" he asked, speeding up to get around an old truck loaded with chicken crates.

"We're getting better at this, Elijah." There was a lightness in her voice that made him want to smile.

"At what?"

"Reading each other. You knew I wanted an explanation. I knew you didn't want me to press you for information. So I waited."

Her observation made him nervous. He knew getting close to Abigail wasn't wise.

"Are you this good at understanding all your patients?" he asked, trying to sound as casual as he could.

His question seemed to take her by surprise. "I'm..." A frown knitted her brow. "I do well with my patients."

The hesitation in her voice sent off warning signals in his brain. "And who do you have a problem with?"

She whipped around to face him. "What do you mean?"

"I mean, who is it you don't get along well with?"

She opened her mouth to protest.

"You've gone to great length to give me your answers. They've been exact. In my line of work, you learn to be cautious of precise responses. What I try to do is understand the meaning behind a person's answer, and not just listen to the words."

She bit her bottom lip, then a chuckle followed.

"I see I've hit the nail on the head."

Lifting one brow, she asked, "Are you always so annoy—perceptive?"

He shrugged. "It's what I do for a living, Abigail. I look for those cracks in what people say and do." If she thought she could get him off the point by diverting his attention, she was in for a shock. "Now, you want to answer my question?"

She lifted her shoulder in what was meant to be a careless gesture. It was ruined by the frown on her face. "I'm not very good in a hospital setting. I prefer to work out among the public."

He didn't say anything.

She glanced out at the mountains.

"What is it about hospitals that you don't like?"

"Nothing," she answered too quickly.

Again he waited for her, allowing the time to lengthen. Finally, when he saw her shoulders relax, he asked, "Maybe it's the doctors you don't like?"

Her head jerked around and she stared at him.

"No," he added after a moment. "I don't think it's all doctors that bother you. Just the ones who act as if they have divine rights."

Her jaw dropped open, and he knew he'd found the compelling factor that put her in the field.

"How did you know that?" she asked, awe in her voice. She leaned close. "You aren't a mind reader, are you?"

A chuckle escaped his mouth. "No, I just used a little logic. The times I've been in the hospital, I've witnessed a couple of nasty scenes when a doctor dressed down a nurse. After spending several days with you, I can see that you might have a problem with that attitude."

"I don't have a problem with authority. Requiring blind obedience is what bothers me."

"You didn't have to confess that, Abigail. I already

knew that was one of your—uh—quirks from first-hand experience.''

She snorted. ''I believe in the chain of command, and it's the doctor's ultimate responsibility to see to his patient's welfare.'' There was more animation in her voice than he had heard before. No, he corrected himself, what it was was passion. ''But I also have a problem with doctors not listening to a nurse who's seen the results of what they have ordered in the way of medication.''

She paused and pursed her lips.

''You might as well tell me the whole story.''

''I'm surprised you don't already know.''

He threw her a look that said he didn't much appreciate the barb.

She shook her head. ''The final straw came when a certain doctor ordered a medication that I had warned him the patient had not responded well to when it was given in a lower dosage. When the doctor didn't change it, I complained and was told I wasn't the one who went to medical school. When the patient had a bad reaction, the doctor and I went toe-to-toe. The woman survived. My supervisor backed me. The doctor continued to practice in that hospital, but I refused to be the nurse for any of his patients.''

''I bet that went over like a dog at a cat-lovers' convention.''

Her expression turned from remote to humorous. ''My supervisor told me about the position as a visiting nurse in the Smoky Mountains. I had completed all the requirements to be a nurse-practitioner and was just waiting for an opening. She thought I would be perfect for the job.'' She tried to smother the laugh that bubbled up.

"What are you not sharing with me? I certainly could use a good laugh right about now."

His reminder of their situation sobered her. "When I applied for the job and was accepted, my supervisor nearly wept for joy. The doctor who had goofed had been driving everyone crazy, trying to get me fired, but no one wanted to fire me. So they were caught between the two of us."

He could imagine how miserable that doctor had made her life.

"It was heaven-sent, that job," she continued. "My mountain folk are wonderful. They may not be rich by the world's standards, but heart-wise, those people are some of the wealthiest I know."

He knew about being poor. He knew about not having a family, but he knew nothing of what she was talking about.

"So it's safe to say that you love your job."

Her face lit up with her enthusiasm. "Yes. What makes everything so extra special is the mountains, themselves. I love the weather there. It's cool and crisp."

"Unlike the Amazon."

Shyly, her eyes met his. "Yeah, in the beginning, that was the best part of being in the mountains."

"And here I thought it was not working with that doctor," he teased.

A flush crept up her cheeks. "And I mistakenly thought that you didn't know how to tease anyone."

His actions surprised him as much as it had her. It was unusual for him to joke with people, but with Abigail, he found himself doing things he'd never done before. Trudging through the jungle topped the list of those unique experiences.

"I'm full of surprises."

"You underestimate yourself, Elijah."

He smiled at her reply.

"Do you know what the best thing I discovered here in the States is?"

"No."

"The seasons."

The breathless quality in her voice led him to think about other things.

"In the Amazon, there's the rainy and dry seasons. Here, it's wonderful. Autumn was a shock to me. To see the leaves change colors, blazing with yellows, oranges and reds. And there's a crisp smell in the air that makes you think of pumpkins and hot apple cider and chilly days." Her eyes sparkled with excitement. "It was like a miracle the first time I ever experienced snow. I stood out in the storm, with my face lifted to the sky and my tongue hanging out, trying to taste that white stuff."

He could see it. A teenage Abigail with her face turned to the sky. All snow meant to him was that the work on the farm changed. He never thought about it as a miracle, just as more work that had to be done. Abigail's view of the world was captivating.

He stared at the darkening horizon, then reached down and turned on the headlights. This mission had proved to be the biggest surprise of all. He didn't know which had thrown him more, knowing that his boss was a double agent, or the fact that he'd had to marry Abigail to get the mission completed.

All day he had fought thoughts of what had happened between him and Abigail last night. Now the images and impressions of their time together filled his head. He'd been with his share of women over the years. He'd always appreciated sex, realized that it was an instinct built into a man that needed to be attended to. But he'd always been able to walk away from the encounters. That gut feeling of his that usually proved to be right was telling him he wouldn't be able to walk away this time. If he did, he would lose a part of his soul.

He glanced over at Abigail. Her eyes had fluttered closed. It had been a hell of a day, ranking right up there with the day he'd been hauled off the farm and plunged into the world of Social Services. Turning his thoughts away from that grim time, he wished they were at their final destination so he could join Abigail in that netherworld of sleep.

The state highway merged with Interstate 25. He glanced at his map and guessed it would take another forty minutes for them to cover the distance to the cabin.

He thought about the briefcase in the back seat. As soon as he had a little sleep, Elijah planned to review again the evidence gathered against Neil. He hadn't taken it all in the last time he read the documents. His memories and feelings had kept interfering with his judgment. If Terrence wasn't there, he also planned to comb through the newspapers that he'd picked up at the store, and try to glean from them where Terrence might have been sent. It was a long shot, but there weren't too many options left open for him.

Besides, this time it wasn't only his skin on the line. He was Abigail's only hope.

Elijah stopped in the small town of Truchas north of Santa Fe. He wanted to find a phone and make sure of Terrence's cabin's location before he drove through to it. Elijah never liked to go into a situation without a backup plan.

His college roommate, Ted Carter, also had a house in this region of the country, in southern Colorado. Elijah had kept in contact with Ted, his first roommate and one of the handful of friends he'd made. Over the years, he and Ted had gotten together and kept abreast of what was happening in each other's life. Elijah never had much to tell, whereas Ted had told Elijah about his marriage and the subsequent birth of his son.

Pulling into a gas station, Elijah cut the engine before the pump. After filling up the tank, he walked into the convenience store, and noted the telephones at the back of the store.

"That will be eighteen fifty-nine," the clerk said.

Elijah handed him a twenty.

"You passing through?" the old man behind the counter asked, handing back Elijah's change.

Elijah didn't want to answer, but he knew that he might be showing up at the store several times in the next few days and didn't want to give this guy any reason to wonder.

"No. The missus and I are staying at a friend's cabin for a few days of rest. He's supposed to meet us there."

The old man eyed Elijah. "Which cabin might that be?"

It was foreign to Elijah to tell anyone what his plans were when he was in the field, but the old guy, by his simple curiosity, had neatly backed him into a corner. It would be unfriendly to tell him to mind his own business. Being friendly was a trait of the people who lived in this remote area and depended on one another.

"We're heading to a cabin just north of here." He hoped the old man would accept that answer.

"Whose cabin you looking for? The Mayer, Downing, Roades or the Rosas cabin?"

Still Elijah was reluctant to say anything.

"If I know, I'll tell the deputy that you're staying there. That way he won't get worried when he sees a light on in the place. There's been a rash of robberies around here. So we're extra careful with strangers."

Before Elijah could answer, the door opened and a highway patrol officer strolled in.

"Hey, Bill, how's it going?" the clerk asked.

"There's been another burglary. The Downing cabin was hit. TV and VCR were stolen."

The old man looked at Elijah. "This here young man is driving to—"

"Terrence Roades's cabin."

The officer nodded. "You a good friend of Terry's?"

"We work together," Elijah answered. "He's supposed to meet us here. I've visited before, right after Terry's marriage."

The patrolman grabbed a candy bar and set it on the counter. "Terrence is sure proud of that little guy of his."

From the neutral expression on the old man's and the officer's faces, Elijah knew that he was being tested. They were wanting to see if Elijah corrected what the officer said.

"And he's nuts about his twin daughter, too," Elijah added casually.

The officer smiled broadly. "Guess you know Terry."

Elijah nodded. "Can't be too careful."

The door opened again, and Abigail entered the store. She smiled easily at the man behind the counter and the officer. "Good evening."

"Howdy. How are you this evening?" the old man asked.

"Fine," she answered. "The weather is beautiful. So dry."

Elijah had to bite back a smile.

"Aren't you a little thirsty?" she casually asked Elijah. She didn't wait for him to answer but walked to the floor-to-ceiling refrigerator, opened the door and pulled out a Pepsi. "Would you like one?"

He shook his head.

The man rang up the sale. "Your husband was just telling me that you're going to Terrence Roades's cabin."

Elijah held his breath, wondering how Abigail would react to the man's statement. She didn't look at him. Instead, she kept her gaze on the old man.

She leaned forward. "Did he tell you that it was our honeymoon?"

The officer looked at them. The old man's eyebrows lifted. "No, he didn't."

She threw a glance over her shoulder, a shy smile on her lips. "Well, it is. We were just married a couple of days ago and wanted some time to be alone with each other. Elijah remembered his friend's place in the mountains and called to ask if we could use it."

"But didn't you say Terry was going to be there?" the old man asked.

Elijah shrugged. "Yes, they're going to join us, but they weren't sure when they could get away. Personally, I hope it takes them a couple of days at least."

The state trooper and clerk looked at each other and grinned in understanding.

"I hope you like the mountains," the old man offered.

A broad smile curved Abigail's mouth. "Elijah knows I love the mountains. This is a special treat for me."

The clerk gave Elijah an approving nod, then handed the purchase to Abigail. "Good luck."

The officer looked at her left hand and raised his brow. "He didn't buy you a ring?"

"Well, if you want the truth, officer, we kinda did it on the spur of the moment. We decided to get rings when we went home. Personally, I'm holding out for a big diamond."

Both the old man and officer smiled at her.

"Don't settle for less," the old man said.

Two teenage girls came into the store, grinning and laughing. "Hi, George, Officer Winston," one of them called. They pulled two soft drinks from the cooler, then slapped them down on the counter.

Elijah decided they'd exposed their plans to enough people. He slipped his arm through hers and pulled her close. "C'mon, sweetheart, let's go." He said it loud enough for both George and Officer Winston to hear. As they pushed open the door, he stole a glance at the group by the counter. Both of the men were trying to bite back smiles, and the teenagers were giving him and Abigail longing glances. Whispers passed among the group.

"Hell," he growled as he escorted Abigail to the

car. A sense of dread settled in Elijah's stomach. At this rate, the entire population of this part of the state would know that he and Abigail were here. Hell, why didn't they just take out an ad in the local newspaper?

"I hope I didn't mess up anything in there," Abigail said as they were driving away. "I can only plead that when I realized I wasn't going to get a Pepsi for the next several days, I decided to go for it while I could." She shrugged and gave him a flirtatious smile. It was odd. Other women had flashed him that same smile, but it hadn't gone through him like fire.

"You did fine. That line about being on our honeymoon was just the ticket."

They truth of the statement hung in the air between them.

She stiffened and looked out the window. He could've bitten his tongue for reminding her that her honeymoon was being spent with a stranger.

She popped the tab on the can and took a deep swallow. "Ah, that is so-o-o good."

"You're a caffeine junky?" He shook his head in amusement. "So you do have faults."

Shock was in her eyes when she looked at him. "Why would you think I didn't have faults?"

He fingered the steering wheel. "You being raised like you were."

She gaped at him. "What does that have to do with anything?"

"Well, if your folks were missionaries—"

Laughter erupted from her. When she could talk, she said, "Oh, Elijah, one's got nothing to do with the other. Some of the wildest kids I knew were the children of missionaries. And then there were—"

"What?" he asked, curious as to what she was going to say.

"Nothing." She took another swig of her drink. It became obvious from the way she was turned away from him and looking out at the dark silhouettes of the mountains that she wasn't going to expand on her point. "Were you worried about what I would say in the store?"

She had pegged him again. It was getting ridiculous how well she read him. "The thought had crossed my mind."

"A man of understatement. I'll keep that in mind."

Elijah took the third cutoff from the road and drove up the hill to where a cabin stood. He parked in the gravel driveway and cut the engine, but left the lights on since there was no other light source on this moonless night. From the darkness of the cabin, it looked like his guess had gone bust. Terrence wasn't here.

"This is it," Elijah said.

She studied the house, then turned to him. "It looks like your boss isn't here."

"'Pears so."

He hopped out of the car and walked up the porch steps, followed by Abigail. At the far corner of the deck were several dirt-filled clay pots. Elijah ran his fingers through the smallest pot and fished out a key he knew was there. He opened the door and flipped on the light switch by the door. Several lamps came on. "Since Terrence became a father, he decided that this cabin needed electricity. When the power company put lines out in this part of the mountains, Terrence was the first one to get hooked up."

Abigail glanced around the cozy living room-kitchen. Two baby swings stood in the far corner. "I see your friend has been here since he had children."

"Yeah. Let's get the groceries inside," Elijah said.

They walked back outside. Between them, they brought in the groceries and their luggage. He set Abigail's backpack in the bedroom. The double bed was now flanked by two cribs.

Elijah debated whether he should leave his backpack in the bedroom, or if he should leave it next to the sofa. What was going to happen this night occupied his mind. He shook off the thought and left his backpack by the door, before joining Abigail in the kitchen.

She had unloaded the food and was putting it away. She located a pitcher and made some of the instant tea. "Do you want some?"

"Not right now."

"Oh." Abigail appeared nervous. "I'm going to take a shower, then go on to bed."

He met her gaze. His hand came up and cupped her chin. "I don't plan on seducing you tonight, Abigail. You can relax."

The smile that curved her lips was poignant. "I'm not worried about you attacking me, Elijah."

Carefully he studied her. "What is it that has you worried?"

Her lips trembled. "I guess I'm afraid that you won't."

She didn't wait for his reaction, but headed toward the bedroom. She had almost reached the door when he caught her arm and turned her to face him.

"Abigail..." He didn't know what he intended to say, but it was the intense longing in her eyes that did him in. His lips came down on hers and devoured them. In her arms, a lifetime of being alone vanished as if it had never been.

Moaning, she opened her mouth, inviting him to taste her. His hands slid up her arms, cradling her head, turning it to deepen the kiss. Her hands clutched his arms, then reached for the buttons on his shirt. One popped off and he distantly heard it fall on the floor.

When her palms rested on his chest, the heat burned through his muscles. He paused and rested his forehead against hers. When he looked at her, in her eyes was the welcome that he needed.

They shed their clothes as they moved to the bed. Elijah pulled back the covers and pulled her down onto the bed with him. There was a need driving him, the one that he'd ruthlessly ignored throughout the past day.

Abigail seemed driven by that same urgency, eagerly responding to his touches, gliding her hands over his skin. Finally, when they were both mindless with want, he covered her with his body and entered her.

This time the sense of coming home was stronger. The bond that had been forged the first time they made love was reinforced. When he plunged into that world of delight, Abigail was there with him, crying out her pleasure.

When he could catch his breath, he rolled onto his side and gathered Abigail close. His last thought before slipping into a deep sleep was that he liked coming home.

Abigail listened to Elijah's deep and even breathing. This time with him had been even more incredible than before, if that were possible. Last night after they had made love, she'd lain awake, staring out into the darkness, wondering why Elijah had retreated with such stunning speed. What had she done? Or, as she finally decided, what demon was he wrestling with?

From the instant she had awakened this morning in Venezuela, events had moved so quickly, much like a cannon barrage, that she and Elijah had been left scrambling to keep ahead of things. The plane ride from Venezuela and then the one from Houston to Albuquerque had given her time to think about what had happened between her and Elijah. They had shared something special. Unique.

Her father had told her that in days gone by weddings were more of a covenant between two families, each pledging aid and support to the other in case of attack and disaster. In an odd way, she and Elijah were aiding each other until they could find a way out of this mess.

A bond had sprung between them. They were on the same team, fighting for the same goal. Although she knew Elijah's agenda from the beginning, knew he was using her to get to his plane, it didn't seem to make a hill-of-beans' worth of difference.

Whatever this thing was that existed between her and Elijah, it certainly was spectacular. She grinned at the thought of how inadequate a word that was to describe what had occurred. More than feelings and emotions, her entire being was involved. All day, she felt as if there was a new understanding between them.

She grinned when she remembered how Elijah had guessed the reason she didn't work in a hospital anymore. She could see why he was good at his job. He was very observant. He did a lot of looking and thinking. She didn't think the man ever did anything on the spur of the moment or half-cocked.

Which meant that this interlude tonight had affected him as deeply as it had her. The question remained—what were they going to do about it? Could she see Elijah spending time on her mountain in Kentucky?

No, she couldn't see him being happy there in the relaxed atmosphere of the mountains. There was a driving force in Elijah that needed an outlet. He channeled it well in his world of deals and double-deals. She sensed he enjoyed the challenge of matching wits with those on the other side.

Since Elijah probably couldn't function in her rural world, could she move to Virginia again and work in a city hospital? The thought sent a chill through her. She couldn't go back to that way of nursing again. So where did that leave them?

You're being a bit premature, she told herself. Although she was sure Elijah had been deeply affected by their lovemaking, that didn't mean that he wanted a real marriage to her. As a matter of fact, he had said nothing about the future. Said nothing about how he felt about her.

Of course, they still were in the midst of a terrible mess. Although Elijah hadn't told her too much about his boss, she had heard his distress when he talked about the situation.

So where did that leave her? That left her wanting to believe there was a future for them, but not confident about that reality.

She closed her eyes and tried to block out her doubt. She didn't succeed.

The soft moan in his ear woke Elijah. Instantly, he was aware of his surroundings. He was in Terrence's cabin in New Mexico. He and Abigail were running from his boss. And Abigail was lying next to him, her slight form pressed against his side.

Well, his resolve not to bed her again had vanished like the fog under a glaring sun. What was wrong with him that he couldn't resist temptation? Why couldn't he concentrate on what Neil had done instead of on what Abigail felt like in his arms?

And yet, he couldn't regret making love to her last night. Or the night before that. It was as if some part of him that had been missing was suddenly discovered. And it felt good. Too good to give up. So where did that leave them?

Didn't he know from his father's example that he was no good with relationships? Hadn't he always vowed not to make the same mistakes his father made?

And yet—

His arm tightened around Abigail's shoulders. She snuggled confidently against him. Odd, in spite of the unusual story he'd had when he showed up at her door, she had trusted him enough to come with him. Although she was wary of going back to the jungle, she'd done it, anyway. That was courage, and he admired her for it. Oh, she didn't follow blindly. She had an annoying habit of wanting to know why they were doing what they were doing. She'd followed his orders. Then when they had a moment's pause, she'd grilled him. She would've made a great general.

He rested his cheek on the top of her head.

The question now remained, could he keep her safe while he tried to get the information on his boss to Terrence? Seeing in black and white the name of the man who had tipped the East Germans on to his first mission had ripped a hole in his soul, one he didn't know how to deal with. Neil had recruited him, been a friend while he was going through CIA training, been like a big brother to him over the years. It was a bitter truth to learn Neil had been responsible for the failure of his first covert mission.

Where was Terrence? Elijah didn't believe that Terrence had suddenly dropped all the burning issues he was handling at the office and gone on a vacation. So what had happened and where had he gone? And was there anyone else in the agency who would be able to interpret those papers? There had only been Terrence, Neil and himself at the meeting to discuss buying the papers from the East German. They had kept it very hush-hush because they didn't want to warn the mole.

Elijah wanted to laugh. They were trying so hard to keep this project low-key and close to the vest. What had they done? Warned the very individual they were after.

And of course there was Jerry, who was dead. And it appeared that Neil was going to get rid of all those who knew about his "activities."

Including Abby.

That meant that they needed to find Terrence and quick.

With a light kiss on Abigail's forehead, Elijah slipped out of bed and padded into the living room. The lights were still on, and their clothes were scattered in a path from the couch to the bed. They'd been in a hurry.

He smiled as he collected his things and slipped on his slacks. As he pulled on his shirt, he noticed it was now missing two buttons. Grinning, he remembered Abigail's actions. He tucked his shirt into his pants, then picked up Abby's things and put them on the chair in the bedroom.

Looking down into her peaceful face, Elijah wanted to forget about looking through the newspapers he'd bought yesterday. He wanted to shed his clothes and join Abigail again. He fought the urge and walked into the living room. The sun was cresting the mountains.

Never before had he had this reaction to lovemaking. But a lot of things in his life had changed since Abigail entered it. Or rather since he entered her life. And what were they going to do when this mess was over? Would they both be alive?

The thought that he was the one who had drawn Abigail into this mess was the motivation he needed to spur him into action. He retrieved the newspapers from the coffee table where he had set them last night, then walked into the kitchen and began to make some coffee.

Chapter 12

A sense of well-being enfolded Abigail as she became aware of her surroundings. She stretched under the sheet and abruptly discovered she wasn't wearing anything.

Her eyes shot open, and she stared at the beamed ceiling, then glanced over her shoulder and saw the baby crib. With blinding clarity she remembered where she was and what had happened.

She moaned and buried her head in the pillow. Oh, my, she thought, she certainly had been uninhibited last night. No one would ever suspect that she was a rather prudish individual who always went by the rules. If she told Elijah that, he probably wouldn't believe her. Or maybe he would.

She was in love. Admitting the truth to herself eased her mind. No matter that Elijah had come to her with the purpose of using her for his mission. Things had changed between them. She realized that, but wondered if he did. And of course, with everything crashing down around them, he didn't have time to think.

She scanned the room, looking for signs of Elijah. Her clothes were draped over a chair in the corner. But he was nowhere to be seen. Scrambling out of bed, she snatched her things from the chair and raced into the bathroom. It would be easier to face him if she was dressed.

After throwing on her clothes, she washed her face and brushed her hair. After brushing her teeth, she felt as ready as she could be to face Elijah.

She walked slowly into the living room and smelled the coffee. Stopping at the entrance to the kitchen, she noted that Elijah was sitting at the table reading a paper.

"I usually read the comics first," Abigail said as she walked into the kitchen.

He glanced up from the article he'd been reading. "Normally, I do, too, but today I needed to see if there were any clues as to where Terrence might have gone."

She remembered the talk they'd had yesterday about him combing through the papers. She grabbed a mug from the shelf and poured herself some coffee. The taste was strong and smooth. "You make a mean cup of coffee, Elijah."

"It's not as good as we had in Brazil, but—" He shrugged.

"I faced that dilemma before. You take what you can get and be grateful."

He studied her. "That's a good attitude."

She glanced at the three papers. "You normally read this many papers?"

"No. Normally I just read the Washington paper. But I wanted to see if there's something reported that might point me in the right direction."

Raising her eyebrow, she gave him a skeptical look. "You can do that from the newspaper?"

A reproving glint appeared in his eye. "Abigail, I'm a CIA control officer. Of course I can do that."

She laughed. "Can you part the Red Sea, too?"

"I'm surprised at you, Abigail. That was Moses who parted the Red Sea, not Elijah."

Her eyes grew wide. He had her there. "Huh—I didn't think you'd know," she admitted.

"Never try to out bluff a CIA control officer." Although his tone was teasing, she knew his sentiment was right on the mark.

"Come here and I'll show you."

She stepped to his side. He pointed to an article on an outbreak of measles in Kazakhstan, where the author of the piece stated that the president planned to visit next month.

Abigail read the article, then looked at Elijah. "What am I to gather from this?"

"If the president plans to go to this area, they need an advance team for security and other things. This outbreak of measles might mean that Terrence needed to go to check things out. Maybe medical teams were being sent to the affected areas. I don't know, but my money's on Kazakhstan. Also, I believe the president hasn't had measles."

"You got all that from that article?"

"It's an educated guess, based on my previous experience."

"I guess that makes sense."

"I need to find Terrence."

"Couldn't you go to someone else in the agency with your proof?"

"I could if I could get close enough to offer it to them. But I'm sure Neil's already blackened my name. At this point, it's his word against mine. And he'll generate evidence, I'm sure. Only Terrence can vouch that we sent Jerry to get this evidence."

Elijah eyes went dark, and she knew he was hurting from the treachery. She rested her hand on his and squeezed.

"Betrayal by an associate is never easy to deal with. It hurts."

"He was more than just an associate. Neil was one of the few people I could count on. When I was in the field, I reported to him, passed him my information. He was the one who got me out of several sticky situations." His eyes were filled with pain. "It's hard to believe that he would sell out his country and his friends." He shook his head. "We lost a number of agents in Eastern Europe because of Neil's actions."

She wanted to gather him into her arms and shield him from the pain as he had done for her back in the jungle. His presence, his strength and warmth had seen her through that dark time, but from his posture, it was clear he was beyond her at this moment.

"You hungry?" she asked, trying to divert him from his grim thoughts.

"I was hoping you'd volunteer to make breakfast. I can cook, but I usually eat out and spare my stomach the grief."

"You're behind the times, Elijah. The new, modern male should know his way around the kitchen."

He pierced her with an intense stare. "I'm not modern."

"A balder truth hasn't been spoken," she grumbled.

A shout of laughter burst from his mouth. "You've got me pegged, Abby." Suddenly, there was a serious light in his eye, and that electric connection that flowed between them sparked. She was tempted to throw herself into his arms and burrow into his strength and let the world pass them by.

Her impulse shocked her. Since when had she taken the easiest path? She'd never hidden behind someone else's strength. But with Elijah, she was as lost as a lamb.

"Uh—how about I scramble us some eggs? And you can make the toast."

"That I can do."

They worked quickly and easily together, as if they had done this a thousand times. And Abigail found herself wanting to experience such compatibility again and again with Elijah.

The realization that this marriage had become the real thing, not just a convenience to get the job done hit her. At least it felt that way for her. But what about Elijah?

"Is everything all right?"

His voice snapped her out of her musing. "Yes."

He handed her two plates. She dished out the eggs while he put the toast on the table.

When they sat down, she saw that Elijah had put salt, pepper and a jar of *picante* sauce in the middle of the table.

Abigail eyed him. "Where did you find that?" She pointed to the sauce.

"I knew Terrence always has some. It adds flavor

to the eggs." He then spooned a large amount of salsa on his eggs. "Would you like some?"

"No, I like to taste my eggs."

Cocking his brow, he said, "And here I thought you were an adventurous soul." He took several forkfuls of egg.

"There's a difference between being adventurous and being independent," she explained.

Leaning back in his chair, he asked, "Oh, how are they different?"

She thought about it a moment. "Well, I like my independence, depending on no one but myself, directing my own future. But it's a sure future. I don't take unnecessary risks. Being adventurous is betting on the unknown, willing to jump when you don't know if someone is there to catch you."

Her words seemed to put a damper on their conversation. Elijah stood and took his plate to the sink, then poured himself a second cup of coffee. She joined him by the stove. Before she could do anything, he picked up the coffeepot and filled her cup. She didn't move away, instead drank her coffee leisurely.

"After we do the breakfast dishes, why don't we go for a walk? I've got time before I'm due to call Jon."

"We?"

He nodded

"Really, you ought to have to do the dishes by yourself, Elijah, since I cooked."

His eyes twinkled with merriment. It was incredible what joy did to his features. "Who worked out this system?"

"You don't want to be fair and share the work? What kind of nineties-kind-of-guy are you?"

"I'm the kind of guy who always eats out."

She shook her head. "I hate to think of the condition of your apartment."

They both sobered at the thought. There were still things about each other that they didn't know. Abigail's heart reminded her of the trauma of Neil's deception that Elijah was coping with.

"Hey, I'm a bighearted individual and will help. You have your choice of washing or drying."

"How about if I dry the dishes and you wash?" he asked. "My skills are better in the drying department."

If his skills in that area where half as good as his lovemaking, she was going to enjoy dishes.

It was amazing how quickly the dishes got done. True to his word, Elijah was handy with a dish towel. He also put away the dishes as he dried them. A feat, he told her, that his sister had never managed.

"My sister used to dry the dishes, but she was still too small to put things away." There was a quiet sadness in his words. He quickly covered up his pain by flashing her a dazzling smile. "This is how I supplemented my income in college."

"By cooking?" she teased, wanting to move away from the awkward moment.

Leaning back against the counter, he folded his arms over his chest. "No, by washing dishes at an Italian restaurant close to the campus. It was a great job because Mario fed me. And I could put away a lot of pasta. It was heaven."

She handed him another plate. "And you didn't bother with learning how to cook?"

"Why? Mario didn't want to share his recipes, and I didn't want to learn to cook. But I can bus a table like nobody's business. After several months, I moved up to waiting tables. The money was better and I still got fed."

She handed him the skillet and pulled the stopper in the sink. "So what do you do now to feed yourself?"

"I eat out. A lot. All I have in my apartment is a jar of instant coffee."

She shivered. "What an awful thought."

He paused in drying the skillet. "What?" he softly asked.

"Instant coffee. It gives me the willies just thinking about it."

"You, Abigail McGee, are a snob." He said it in such a lighthearted manner that there was no sting.

"No, you are mistaken." She folded the dishcloth and hung it over the faucet. "What I am is a connoisseur."

"Is that what it's called now?" he replied in a deadpan tone.

She felt a bubble of laughter work its way up until it burst from her lips. "I don't believe it. You surprise me every time when you tease me."

He grinned. "I think, Abigail, that you have uncovered a part of me that no one ever knew existed. Even me."

Glancing down at his watch, he said, "I have a couple of hours before I need to call Jon. Let's take that walk."

"I'd like that."

The cabin was perched on the side of a mountain. In the bright light of day, the view was spectacular. Below them in the valley, a creek bubbled over the rocks in its path. The trees were brilliant in their red, gold and orange colors of fall. Combined with that feast for the eyes, the tangy smell of pine trees filled the air.

Abigail took a deep breath, savoring the fragrances. "I often think this is what heaven must be like."

"Heaven?" Elijah gave her a blank stare.

"Haven't you ever wondered what heaven is like?" she asked, curious.

From his expression, this was a new concept for him. "No. I've been too busy trying to take care of today to wonder about someday." There'd been a slight hesitation in his "no."

"I don't believe you."

He stopped dead, staring at her. "What makes you say that?"

She tried to sound casual. "I just have this feeling that maybe you had thought about heaven."

"Would you like a job, Abigail? I could use someone as perceptive as you."

"No, I don't want another job. I'm happy doing what I do." She wondered why she could so keenly read Elijah. It was a new experience for her. Oh, she was perceptive about people's motivation. But with Elijah, it was like being on the same radio frequency with him. "Now, tell me the truth. Have you ever thought about heaven?"

"And tenacious." He grinned.

"I've dealt with a lot of stubborn males, and I've generally been able to out-stubborn them," Abigail commented.

"That, I don't doubt for an instant."

She folded her arms under her breasts. His gaze followed. The heat from his eyes made her mouth go dry. In a toe-to-toe confrontation, she had to admit that Elijah could win hands down. Clearing her throat, she turned and began walking down the driveway.

A chuckle sounded behind her.

In a couple of steps he caught up with her and grabbed her hand. "Heaven was a subject I never dwelt on. I couldn't fathom it. And didn't try."

"You didn't try to imagine it?" she asked, incredulous at his answer. Her young life had been filled with thoughts of a time to come.

"All I tried to imagine was where my next meal was coming from," he answered with a shrug.

She still didn't believe him. There was a richness in him that came from a productive imagination. The question was, would he ever share that with her? Did they have enough time together to build enough trust between them so that he would willingly share with her? "You should've met my dad. He could've made you see the place. He could paint a vivid picture with his words."

"And I have the feeling that you asked questions about it."

She shrugged. "If you're asking if I was curious as a child, I'll admit I was. I mean, when you're living in the jungle with only books for entertainment, you discover a reserve of creativity."

His laugh floated on the air. "I don't doubt that even if you hadn't lived in the jungle, you would've developed a creative imagination."

"And why do you say that?"

"It's a feeling I have."

She hoped he'd continue. "Why do you have that feeling, Elijah?"

He slanted her a penetrating look, trying to discern the motivation behind her question. "Because, I see...I had a lot of time as a kid and teenager to myself."

He didn't have to mention his drunken father or missing mother. The imagination he accused her of having took over. The thought nearly broke her heart.

He looked out over the valley. "Books were worlds that took me away from the dreariness of the here and now. And I dreamed."

"What did you dream about?"

He shrugged again.

Abigail knew she'd breached the wall surrounding his heart. She wanted to shout for joy, but decided that if she pushed, Elijah would clam up on her again and try to withdraw. "This place is really beautiful," she said, trying to bring the conversation back to what they started talking about.

Elijah glanced around. "I had always heard Terrence speak about this place. Finally, I came out one year to visit my college roommate and came by here. I found this place...peaceful."

From the way he said it, "peaceful" wasn't a state he often experienced.

She wanted to know more about the man who was her husband. "Do you have any hobbies?"

A smile curved his mouth. "No. What I do is a full-time job, leaving little time to do anything else."

"I can't believe that. We all have to have something in our lives apart from work."

"And do you have a hobby?" he shot back.

"Several."

"You going to tell me?"

She considered being as closemouthed as he, but then decided she didn't like playing that game of keeping everything close to her. She was the only one who suffered when she tried to live according to someone's rules. "I crochet and sew."

"I don't think that crocheting is right for me."

"There are several professional football players who knit and crochet."

He shook his head. "I don't care who does it. I don't." There was a finality to his tone that told her not to waste her breath trying to argue anymore.

"I wasn't suggesting you do. Just giving you examples of hobbies."

Silence reigned.

He bent down, picked up a stone and threw it. "I build models."

She fought against the smile trying to burst free. Elijah probably wouldn't appreciate it.

"Why didn't you become a missionary like your parents?" His voice echoed through the trees.

His question startled her. It was the last thing she expected him to ask her. It also irritated her. He was wanting her to bare her soul, yet he didn't want to share anything of himself. "I'll trade you, Elijah. Information for information."

He stopped. There was suspicion in his eyes. "What do you want to know?"

"I'll answer your question if you tell me why you joined the CIA."

After a long pause, he nodded his head. "Okay. But you go first."

Crossing her arms, she murmured, "Now, why aren't I surprised?"

He remained silent, waiting for her to start.

Sighing, she began, "I wasn't cut out to be a missionary. If I ever get married and have children, I want them to be raised in a boring little house in a boring little town here in the U.S.A. with boring parents who go to work and come home every night. Also, I don't want to uproot my kids every couple of years and move them half a world away. I want my children to have friends they don't have to leave. I want them to have a feeling of permanence in their lives. Not to wonder how long it will be before they move again."

She fell silent, wondering if her bitterness rang as loudly in her words as she felt them. One look at Elijah told her they had. But there was a sympathetic light in his eyes. He knew from experience what she was talking about. He waited for her to continue.

Refocusing her mind, she thought about what she wanted Elijah to know. How could she explain her confused heart? "I wanted to help people, also, like my parents. But unlike Mom and Dad, I felt nursing was the field I wanted to go into. I could help people, but come home to the same house every night."

His eyes met hers, and she felt the probing strength of his gaze. He was looking for honesty and truth. She purposely didn't hide her feelings from him.

"My sister felt like I did about being a missionary, and she became a teacher," she added as an afterthought. "We both are homebodies. She doesn't even like to travel to the next town."

"Something tells me that both you and your sister are well-adjusted adults, who give back to the community."

"I won't deny that, but you were wanting to know

why we chose careers different from our parents. That's the reason why."

"And did your parents' deaths in the plane crash have anything to do with your or your sister's decision?"

If he'd stabbed her, he couldn't have surprised her more. She gasped.

He reached for her, but she stepped away from him.

He threw his head back and took a deep breath. "I'm sorry, Abigail. It's the bastard in me that made me ask."

It was startling, but Elijah's question made her face the demons that had been plaguing her since her parents' deaths. Instead of the usual resentment and pain, there was a peace in her heart. Seeing how well the tribe was doing in this changing time had healed a lot of her old wounds. And if Elijah hadn't made her go down to the Amazon and face those ghosts, she never would've known the impact her parents had made.

She touched his arm. "It's a fair question. Yeah, my parents' deaths figured into both mine and my sister's choice of careers. I've been angry for a long time about Mom and Dad's deaths. But you know what, Elijah, going with you to the Amazon put to rest a lot of the pain and anger I felt. Thank you."

She rose up on tiptoes and brushed a kiss across his lips. His arms went around her waist and he pulled her back for another kiss, slow and deep. When he ended the kiss, she rested her head on his shoulder.

"Now, why don't you tell me why you joined the CIA," she softly reminded him.

He chuckled. "I'm learning that I can't slip anything past you."

"We made a deal," she answered.

"Indeed we did." Sitting down on a fallen tree, he tugged her down beside him. Looking out into the valley, he began, "I told you how the Company came to the college where I was going to school. And after I graduated, how I went into the military and worked in MI—military intelligence. I found I was good in that area and decided to apply to the CIA after I got out. I worked in the field for several years, recruiting foreign nationals to gather information that I could pass on to Washington. It was exciting. I was doing something to help my country. I felt…" He seemed embarrassed by his feelings. Clearing his throat, he added, "I could give back. Coming from where I did, I had wonderful opportunities that this country gave me."

"So you're not so different from me," she murmured. When she heard her own voice, she seemed surprised that she'd voiced her thoughts.

"Yeah, in an odd sort of way."

A giggle escaped her lips.

A frown wrinkled his brow. "What do you find so funny?"

"The picture of you as a nurse flashed through my brain." She shrugged. "It just seemed ridiculous. I can just see you the first time you and a doctor had a disagreement."

He grabbed her hand and pulled her into his lap. His fingers caressed her jaw. "You don't think I could do the job?"

She threw back her head and laughed. "I don't doubt you could do the job. It's your temperament that might prove to be a problem for you."

"Why would you say that?"

"Oh, please. You'd flatten the first doctor that

asked you what medical school you attended.'' She shook her head. ''No, I can't see you putting up with that kind of arrogance.''

His hands soothed back the tendrils that had escaped her braid. ''No, I've got no patience for over-inflated egos. And heaven knows that there is a higher percentage of them in Washington than anywhere else in the world, including the medical profession.''

''And you don't deal well with pomposity?'' She tried to keep her tone light, but the fire in Elijah's eyes stole the breath from her lungs.

His fingers continued to stroke her temples. ''No,'' he answered distractedly as he lowered his head toward hers, ''I don't.''

When his lips covered hers, every thought in her brain fled, and she only felt the fire of his kiss. What they were facing faded, and this moment expanded to fill the universe.

Abigail slipped her arm around his neck and abandoned herself to the moment. Elijah pulled back.

''Are you worried about the guy who's looking for us?'' she asked.

''Yeah, I was thinking about Neil.''

''I'm sorry that he betrayed you.''

His hand covered hers. ''After my dad died, I felt lost. There was no one there for me until I met Neil. He guided me through my early years at the CIA. I told him things that I hadn't ever told another soul, not even my college roommate. Neil was the guy I confessed to how much I missed my sister. She had no problem getting adopted once CPS made us available. But I was nine and angry and there was no family that wanted me. I was a handful. Neil helped me face those ghosts.''

She rested her head on his shoulder. "When my parents died, I was mad at heaven for letting them die. Hadn't they sacrificed themselves? It seemed senseless and wrong. But seeing that village now, seeing the results of my parents' work, made me realize that the work they did benefited the villagers. Teaching them to read and write their own language, putting that language into a written form, gave them the tools to keep themselves from being overwhelmed by the modern world.

"In your case, Elijah, be grateful for what Neil did. What he gave you isn't changed by his other actions."

He gave her a startled look. "What do you mean?"

"What Neil did was wrong. But his actions toward you were those of a friend. Didn't he help you to deal with those old ghosts?"

"Yeah."

"Then hold on to the good you can find in this situation. Dwell on it, and not on the betrayal. And I can speak from experience."

"I don't know," he murmured. "I can't even see the end of this mess."

"When I was a kid, I used to dream about a home on the side of a mountain, high and dry. And in this house was a husband who loved me and our babies. The dream was that we'd live in that enchanted place, never moving, and see our grandchildren born there. It kept me happy each time we moved to another location and each time I had to make new friends. I could do what I needed to do because I had a hope of a future that was of my making."

"And you have that house in the mountains, don't

you?'' he said, brushing the back of his hand over her cheek.

"Yes."

There was a wealth of unsaid meaning in her voice. Where was the husband and child in her vision? He guessed he qualified as her husband. And the idea of a child, their child, growing up in that house in the Appalachians, held a wonderful appeal for him.

"Did you have a dream, Elijah, that helped you get through all those foster homes when you were a teenager?" Her voice was soft and seductive, dancing across his nerves.

"Yes," he admitted before he thought. Did he want to open up to Abigail and let her look that deeply into his soul? The only other person he'd opened up to was Neil. And look how that had ended.

But she was his wife, wasn't she? a voice in his head argued. And she seemed to understand him in a way that no other individual had. What did he have to lose?

He closed his eyes, trying to recall the dream. "Sometimes late at night, when I was alone in my bed, I would imagine a white farmhouse with a big swing on the front porch. Inside, there was my family." He paused, realizing with awe that Abigail's house up on the mountain could be described with the words he'd just muttered. "There was a red barn beside it."

He met her gaze, wondering if she saw the parallels between his dream and her reality. There in her eyes was the answer. Yes, she did.

"What else did you see in your dream?" Her voice was a siren song, calling him to tell her what was in his heart. And he felt like Ulysses from Greek mythology, unable to ignore her request.

"There was a big kitchen table where we would all sit, eat, play games. And talk." He stared down at his hands. "My experience was very different from that dream. My mother used to spend the evenings telling my dad how unhappy she was, what she was missing and what we didn't have. Meals were hell."

She laid her hand on his cheek. He jerked his gaze to hers.

"It wasn't your fault, Elijah. It was something in your mother that was lacking, but not you."

"Logically, I know that."

"Then believe it with your heart."

It was tempting to surrender to Abigail's words. "Do you do counseling on the side?"

She grinned, then shrugged. "Give me a break, Elijah. My parents were missionaries. I can't help it if I try to fix everything."

He brushed her cheek with the back of his fingers. "You're amazing. It was a stroke of good fortune that brought you into my life."

Laughter lit her eyes. "And here I thought it was the CIA."

He chuckled. "Sometimes even the CIA gets it right."

His lips covered hers, and he let the feelings building up in him break free of the cage. It was heaven, letting free that which was inside. After several minutes, he rested his forehead against hers. As he sought to find his control, Elijah admitted to himself that he was in hip-deep trouble here. Instead of trying to figure out how he was going to get them out of this mess, considering all the different ways things might go, all he could think about was taking Abigail back to the cabin, laying her on the bed and loving her.

Where was his famous iron control? His single-mindedness that was his hallmark? That man seemed to have been lost somewhere in the jungles of the Amazon. Not only was that individual lost, he didn't have a single idea about what to do with the situation that had developed between him and Abigail. They were married—it didn't matter that it was forced on them. They were wed, the job done by a preacher. And Elijah didn't doubt that Samuel would follow up and file the necessary paperwork with the national government of Brazil.

But it wasn't the marriage that worried him. That could be dealt with easily. No, what bothered him was the bond that had sprung up between him and Abigail. Each time he touched her, made love to her, that bond grew stronger. And his only desire at this point was to continue building that connection.

"We'd better get back to the cabin. It's almost time for me to call Jon."

She nodded and looked away. He felt her confusion as keenly as he felt his own. And he couldn't ignore it. His fingers cupped her chin and brought her gaze to his. "I—"

His throat closed up. He wanted to tell her how he felt, but a lifetime of caution wouldn't allow him to say the words. Instead, his mouth covered hers and he tried to tell her with his lips what was in his heart.

He raised his head and let his arms fall free of her. With a shy smile, she leaned close and brushed her mouth across his, stood, and started walking back to the cabin. As he watched her, for the first time in his life, Elijah felt contentment.

* * *

Elijah slipped the car keys into the front pocket of his jeans. "Why don't you come with me, Abigail? You can talk to whoever is running the cash register, maybe divert their attention."

"I could buy another Pepsi."

"That sounds great." He pulled open the door and waited for her to go before him. As she passed by him, he caught a whiff of the floral scent of her shampoo, making him want to reach out and touch the rich mass of her hair.

It took less than ten minutes for them to get to the crossroads where the little store was located. When they pulled up, Elijah looked at her.

"Are you ready?"

There was a disquiet in her eyes. "Yes, as ready as I'll ever be." She pushed open her door.

The clerk behind the counter was different than last night. He was a teenager.

"Hi," Abigail greeted the youth.

Elijah nodded to the youth, then walked to the back of the store.

Abigail strode over to the glass refrigerator case and took out two drinks. When she set the cans down on the counter, she glanced out of the corner of her eye and made eye contact with Elijah. He smiled at her, trying to silently encourage her to talk to the teenager.

They were a few minutes early for his rendezvous time with Jon, so Elijah called Terrence's cell phone. It was answered on the third ring.

"Hello." Elijah recognized Diane's voice.

"Diane, where's Terrence?"

"Elijah, it's good to hear from you. Terry's been called out of the country on one of those projects you guys do. He left his cell phone with me."

"I tried calling yesterday," Elijah explained.

"Huh—well—it was last night when I discovered one of the twins had put their dad's phone in the swimming pool. I immediately replaced it." She laughed. "It's just one of those unexpected joys of parenthood."

"Do you know when he'll be back?" Elijah asked, hoping against hope that Diane would know.

"Oddly enough, I heard from him this morning. He'll be home late tonight."

"Was he coming in on a commercial flight or military?" Elijah asked.

"He didn't say. But he said I didn't have to bother picking him up."

"Thanks for the help, Diane. If Terrence calls, tell him that I got the evidence we were after." He hung up the phone. Well, at least he knew Terrence would be back within the next few hours.

Maybe Jon had found out something. He dialed Jon's number. It was picked up on the first ring.

"Michaels here," was the no-nonsense greeting.

"What did you find out, Jon?" Elijah asked.

"Well, Terrence's secretary was discreet, but she said that he'd be back in the office tomorrow and I could get my information from him."

"His wife just told me he's flying in late tonight. Do you know where he's coming in? Is it Andrews or Dulles?"

"Andrews. He was going to take a military flight home," Jon answered.

"I don't know how soon I can get out of here. I'll probably have to drive to Albuquerque."

"Why don't you let me go for you, Elijah. I got your package this morning. I could fly into—"

"You've got a family, Jon."

"Only because you hauled my butt out of that wreck in Europe and watched over me until I got well. It's my turn now. Besides, I have a couple of favors to call in from people at Andrews. I think I might be able to talk to Terrence before he lands. I won't be in the line of fire."

Elijah didn't like it, but Jon was in a better position than he was. He was a short drive away from the Dallas airport. Who knew when Elijah could get a flight out of Santa Fe or Albuquerque, and it probably wouldn't be a direct flight. "All right. I'll check in with Lauren at eighteen hundred at your home number to see what your status is."

"I'll warn Lauren. Oh, and by the way, old buddy. I called Jeremy Sanders, my old roommate from training days, with the excuse just to chew the fat. He told me the most amazing story. And you know what that was?"

Elijah knew he wasn't going to like what Jon said. "Shoot."

"You're the bad guy. Shocked everyone. They were whispering about it all morning over coffee."

Elijah cursed.

"I thought that might make your day. Call Lauren at the arranged time."

"Got it."

Elijah hung up. He should feel relieved that things had gone so smoothly, that Jon had volunteered to run interference for him. Of course, Neil had wasted no time in blackening his name.

He wondered if any of his colleagues questioned Neil's assertion.

Chapter 13

Elijah was turned toward the telephone, his back blocking out what he was saying. The teenage clerk looked at him. Wanting to distract the boy, Abigail asked, ''You look like the older gentleman who helped us last night.''

The youth grinned. ''That's my granddad. I work on the weekends when there isn't any school.''

''What grade are you in?''

''I'm a junior this year.'' He rang up the purchase of two Pepsis. ''That's a dollar eight.''

Elijah had just hung up the telephone, but promptly dialed another number.

Abigail fished the money out of her wallet and handed it to the boy. ''Where do you go to school?''

The youth's attention shifted to her. ''There's a high school in Ojo Sarco. That's a few miles north of here.''

Elijah appeared to be finishing up his conversation.

"How many are in your high school?" Abigail asked, praying that everything was all right with Elijah.

"The graduating class this year is seven. There's fifteen of us in my class." He handed her the change.

Abigail put the money in her wallet. "That's better than mine. There were five hundred in mine. You kinda got lost in the crowd."

The youth laughed. "There aren't that many folks in this area, let alone the school."

Elijah joined her. "Are you ready to go?"

"It was nice meeting you—"

"Mike," the clerk supplied.

"Good luck to you." She waited until they were seated in the car, then asked Elijah, "How did it go?"

He started the engine. "Jon was able to talk to Terrence's secretary." He pulled the car onto the road. "She told him that Terrence had gone on a mission for the White House, but that Terrence had just called from Heathrow. He's due back in his office tomorrow."

"So what are we going to do?" Abigail asked.

"We're going to sit tight."

If he had said they were going to the White House and parade around naked she couldn't have been more shocked. "What am I missing here?"

"Jon's going to meet Terrence. He has the copy of the papers I sent him. He didn't say how he was going to get to Terrence, but he will. Jon is amazingly resourceful. What you and I are going to do is drive to Santa Fe and get a cell phone so I can have it at the cabin."

A frown darkened his brow. She knew that he was holding something back. "There's something more."

"Oh, what?"

"When Jon called a friend there at the agency, ostensibly to chew over old times, his friend told him the latest gossip. Seems Neil had discovered who the mole in the agency was who'd been feeding the other side."

She had a sick feeling in her stomach. "Who was it?"

"It, according to Neil, is me."

"We were expecting that."

He glanced at her. "We were. I just wanted to let you know that our expectations had come true."

Her heart seemed to skip a beat. Elijah was, without prompting, telling her what they were facing. He was communicating with her. She reached over, grasped his hand and squeezed it. "Thank you."

"For what?" He looked puzzled.

"For telling me what's going on."

A frown creased his brow. "Thank you for putting you in danger?"

"Don't be so hard on yourself. You can't help what others do."

He frowned, then said, "I knew you'd want to know what we were facing."

"But you volunteered the information this time. We're making progress, Elijah."

He glanced at her. "I guess we are." Then he smiled.

That nagging feeling he had when things weren't right settled in the pit of his stomach and wouldn't go away no matter what argument he used. Something wasn't right.

Elijah had just reached the interstate when he

pulled off onto the side of the road. Running his hand through his hair, he mumbled, "I can't. I can't let him do it."

"What are you talking about?" Abigail asked.

He faced her. "I can't let Jon go alone to Andrews and meet with Terrence. There's a nagging sense of unease...something not right."

There was a fierce light in his eyes. And she knew no matter what she said, it wouldn't change his mind. "Then, I guess we'll need to go to Washington."

"We?" His brow arched.

"Elijah, I understand that you can't let your friend go into this situation alone. I admire that. But I also know that I can't stay here in New Mexico while you're in Washington. I might as well fly home."

He opened his mouth to reply, then closed it. "Okay, Abigail. Let's go back to the cabin and get our things and find us a flight out of here."

Elijah looked around the cozy little house where he and Abby had spent the last twenty-four hours to make sure they hadn't left anything. He felt a stab of envy for his old friend, Terrence. Here he had a home, wife and children. And he was happy.

And then there was Jon, also finding a new and fulfilled life with his wife and daughter.

Elijah hadn't thought that any of that would be possible for him. Now he saw the world in a different light. Possibilities abounded. Possibilities that he'd never even entertained. Now that he'd tasted that fruit, Elijah found himself wanting more. Would it be possible? Abby had told him about her dreams of being a boring parent to her children, and of course she would want a boring man who'd come home every day—not a man with secrets who might have to leave at a moment's notice.

Abigail appeared in the bedroom door. "I think I've got everything." She glanced around the little cabin. "Your friend's lucky." Her gaze meet his. There was a longing there, but he backed away from it.

"He is, and I think he knows it." He stepped close, and, unable to stop himself, he cupped her cheek. "And I envy him."

"Why?"

"Because he's got a future with his wife and children in it."

"And you don't?" Her eyes darkened.

"I don't know." He could see she wanted more from him, but at this point he couldn't give it to her. He wanted to reassure her but didn't want to give her hollow promises like his father had given him. Promises his dad never kept. For Elijah, his word was a sacred bond and he didn't give it lightly. He wanted to explain that to her, but he needed time and that was something they didn't have at the moment.

"C'mon, we need to go."

She started to open her mouth to argue, then closed it and walked to the door. He wished he knew what she had been going to say.

Neil walked into Terrence's office. "Have you heard anything from Terry?" he asked the secretary.

"The embassy in Kazakhstan gave us the green light to proceed with a security detail for the president. The measles outbreak is in the eastern part of the country. It won't affect the president's trip."

"So Terry's coming back?"

"Yeah, just in time to take his wife out for their anniversary. The military transport is due in at Andrews around six tonight."

"Thanks," Neil replied. That gave him a couple of hours to round up some bogus documents to shift the blame onto Elijah. Too bad he couldn't find the bastard and kill him before he could make any waves. But, who knew, maybe Elijah would try to beat him to the airport and show Terrence his documents first. And if Elijah did, he'd be ready for him. He'd also have to get rid of the woman. But that wouldn't be any problem.

Elijah glanced over at Abigail. They were on their first leg of the journey, flying from Albuquerque to Dallas. They would make their connections there. But Elijah didn't want Abigail flying to Knoxville by herself. He wanted her with him until the entire situation was resolved. That sixth sense of his told him something wasn't right.

"I want you to come with me to Washington until we get this thing resolved."

The light that had flared in her eyes went out. "Oh."

"I mean—"

"You don't need to make excuses, Elijah. We didn't plan on what happened to us."

He grabbed her hand in his. "Your safety is utmost in my mind. If you're with me, then I'll know for sure you're all right. It's because of me you're in this mess."

She didn't say anything.

"At least you could argue with me," he grumbled.

"Why? You've put everything in a nutshell. I couldn't say it better myself."

He didn't look happy with her answer. "Abby, I'm lost here. Since my sister and I were separated over twenty years ago, I've been alone. I never planned on falling in love, because I saw how destructive it was for my parents. I built my life around my job, and I did everything based on that."

"And?"

He didn't answer, trying to figure the best way to answer. "Suddenly, the rules that guided my life up to this point don't seem to apply. I feel—"

"Would it help if I told you that in spite of everything, I've fallen in love with you?"

His eyes darkened with passion and his hand cupped her cheek. Softly, he brushed his lips over hers. "I don't believe I'm the man of your dreams, Abby. I'm not the man you dreamt of, or saw coming home every night."

She turned her head away but he saw a single tear run down her cheek. "You're wrong. Love isn't destructive, Elijah, or selfish. It's the greatest motivating factor in this universe. It's also the most precious."

Another tear slid down her cheek. It was like that tear was acid, burning a hole in his heart.

They didn't speak again until they landed in Dallas.

"Why don't you have your ticket changed to Dulles while I call Diane again," Elijah explained as he headed toward the phones.

She wanted to tell Elijah to leave her alone, but he had that steely look in his eyes that said he wasn't going to accept any arguments.

By the time the woman behind the counter had reissued her ticket, Elijah was back. From his thunderous expression, it appeared things weren't going well.

"What's wrong now?"

He didn't bother denying anything. "Terrence called Diane. Today's their anniversary and he called from London to tell her that he'd had to switch to a commercial flight because the air force plane he was on developed engine problems. He said it would be close to midnight when he would be home."

"If he was taking a commercial flight that would mean—"

"That he would land at Dulles, not Andrews. Which means that Jon will miss him." He rubbed the back of his neck. "Of course, if Jon is expecting Terrence to land at Andrews, then maybe Neil is counting on that, too."

"Wouldn't Jon be in danger from Neil?" she asked.

"No. Neil didn't know what agents I was running in Europe. I doubt Neil ever met Jon. When I was hiding him in Europe for two years, no one knew of his existence but me."

Their flight was called and they boarded the plane. As they were taking off, the thoughts of Jon and Neil kept pounding her brain. Abby put down the magazine she was reading. "I don't see why you want your job, Elijah. It su—" She bit off the end of the word. Her eyes were wide with surprise.

After a moment of stunned surprise, Elijah started laughing. Abby joined him. They drew looks from the other passengers.

"You almost said something uncharacteristic for you."

Tears rolled down her face, she was laughing so hard. "I've done a lot of new things since I met you."

"That I don't doubt."

"I'll say this for you, Elijah, I have a much different view of your job now. After living it, your vocabulary is understandable."

"At least we're making progress."

"What do you plan once we arrive at Dulles?" she asked.

"I plan to check and see what time the planes from Heathrow land and be close to those gates."

"So once you give those papers to Terrence this will be over?" she asked.

"What do you mean by 'this'?"

She was surprised that he picked up on her double meaning. She was wanting to know about this mission and about their relationship, their marriage, but she thought that he was so focused on getting to Terrence that he couldn't see beyond that goal. Apparently she was wrong. "I mean about this incident—for lack of a better word." She wouldn't mention their marriage again. He'd already made it clear that it was a mistake.

"After Neil's arrested, it's going to take a while to sort through everything that he compromised. It's going to be a nightmare."

"Oh." She tried to keep the disappointment out of her voice. Her gaze drifted out the window and she stared into the darkness. Stars twinkled in the night sky.

Elijah felt her pain and disappointment keenly. She was wanting things from him that he never thought he could give. And it scared him. Abby wanted someone who came home every night and came from the same background as she did. What did she know of the emptiness that had ruled his life? He'd filled his world with bits of information and was the best at what he did. But the world she opened up for him was so different from the world he knew, that he was afraid to explore this new place. He couldn't help but try to ease her disappointment.

"I remember lying in the grass at my folks' farm and wondering about the stars. What were those worlds like? Was there life?" They were dreams he held closely to himself, never sharing with anyone before now. He wondered how she was going to react.

"It seems logical with all those stars and planets that there's life out there somewhere."

His startled gaze met hers. "You think so?"

"Sure, it makes sense."

"You're a surprise, Abigail."

"Why, because I don't think you're a nutcase for wondering about life in the universe?"

He shrugged.

She turned and gazed out again. "I had a lot of wild ideas as a child that I told my sister, Leah, about. It was nice to be able to share those flights of fancy with someone and not be laughed at."

"I envy you."

"I'll be willing to listen any time you want to talk to me, Elijah." There was a silent invitation in her eyes. One he wanted to answer. But felt inadequate to respond to.

They touched down at Dulles just after eight in the evening. As they stood in the tram that took them from the airplane to the gate, his gaze searched the windows of the terminal, not that he could see much. Once the tram pulled up to the gate, he took Abigail's hand and walked with her into the terminal. Instantly, they walked over to the screens that listed arriving flights. There was one flight listed from London and it arrived at nine-fifteen.

"We have some time to kill. And since I don't want to wait out here in the open, why don't we go to the lounge and get something to drink?" When she gave him a stern look, he replied, "You can have a soft drink."

"Let me visit the ladies' room, then I'll join you."

"All right. I'll be just inside the door."

Elijah went into the lounge and ordered two soft drinks. After ten minutes had passed, he was up and out of his seat, heading for the women's rest room. Something was wrong. His gut was shouting a warning.

He didn't make it. There, sitting beside the entrance, was Abigail with Neil sitting next to her. Her beautiful blue eyes were filled with terror. Elijah could hardly swallow around the knot of fear and anger that lodged in his throat. Elijah didn't doubt for a second that Neil had a gun on her.

"Good, it appears you brought the documents," Neil said, nodding to Elijah's briefcase. "Why don't we go somewhere quiet and discuss things?" Neil's smile was cold, sending chills down Elijah's spine. He felt sure Neil intended to kill both him and Abby. What Elijah needed to do was figure out how he was going to get them out of this mess.

And he'd better be damn quick.

Chapter 14

"I knew it was a mistake sending you after those documents. But I thought the crash in the Amazon would take care of everything," Neil calmly explained as they walked through the terminal.

Elijah's heart was racing. Fear for Abigail pounded through his veins. Neil didn't have anything to lose by killing him and Abigail. He was the reason Abby was facing death now.

"Why'd you do it, Neil?" Elijah asked. "Why'd you sell out your country?"

"While I was working in East Germany, I met a woman. I knew she was working for the other side, but I couldn't stop myself from pursuing her. After the affair ended, I found I liked the money that the other side paid me. It became addictive." He shrugged.

"Did it ever bother you that you sent all those agents to their deaths?"

Neil's eyes were hard. "I liked the money, Elijah. It buys salve for the soul."

Abigail looked at the man. "You're wrong. Money doesn't buy peace."

Neil's brow shot up. "You've found yourself another idealist, haven't you, Elijah. Whoever would've thought the daughter of missionaries and Elijah Kendrick were such soul mates, such goody two-shoes?" He looked from one to the other, then with an evil grin said, "Too bad."

"My first mission in East Germany. You're the one who sold me out, weren't you?" Elijah asked, the question just popping out.

Neil shrugged his shoulders. "I didn't know they'd give you that assignment until too late. Eventually, my East German handlers asked for your identity, Elijah," he quickly added. "I gave it to them. But in the next month, their government came tumbling down."

Elijah stared at Neil. Elijah's mouth opened, then closed, no sound passed his lips.

Tears gathered in Abigail's eyes as she looked from one man to the other. They had been at one time closest of friends. Now...the pain Elijah was experiencing was reflected in his eyes.

Neil frowned. "I tried to stop you, Elijah, before you could get that information." He pressed the gun into Abigail's ribs.

Abby's gaze met Elijah's. They'd faced this same situation in Venezuela and they could work the same trick...maybe. As they were approaching the outside door, she looked at Elijah, hoping he would understand, then collapsed in a heap. Her actions threw Neil off balance, and he pulled back to prevent himself from going down. Elijah wasted no time in tackling

Neil. The gun in Neil's hand went skidding across the floor. Abigail raced after it and ran into a huge man standing in her path. He was reaching down to get the gun. Her breath caught as she looked up at the stranger.

"I'm Jon," he said quickly. Abigail breathed a sigh of relief.

She turned back to see Neil hit Elijah with a stunning blow. Elijah shook the blow off and countered with a series of blows to Neil's face and body, knocking him out cold. Elijah turned around, looking for the gun, when he saw Jon.

"What the hell took you so long?" Elijah asked.

Jon smiled. "You had it under control. You didn't need my help. Besides, I remember you came in about the same time for me and Lauren when we were in London. I thought I'd return the favor."

Elijah replied in terms that made Abigail blush and looked around to see several policemen coming toward them.

"You'd better get out your ID, Elijah," Jon blandly remarked. "We're going to have some explaining to do."

Terrence joined the crowd in the administrator's office, located by airport security. There were a couple of airport security people, D.C. police and more CIA officials.

"I heard that two of my people were up here." Terrence looked at Elijah, then Neil. "Ah, and we have Jon Michaels. Anyone want to explain to me what's going on?" He didn't sound too thrilled.

Since they had brought everyone into this room, Neil hadn't said anything. Elijah and Jon had requested Terrence's presence when he arrived before they did any explaining.

Elijah stood up. "I've got documents with me that will explain everything. I'm sorry, Terry, but Neil's the mole.

"It seems that Neil didn't want you to see them. He was going to dispose of me and Abigail. I'm sure he was going to claim I was the bad guy."

Terrence took a step back, his face paling as he stared at his second-in-command.

"It's not true!" Neil screamed. "It was Elijah. I can show you—"

Jon stepped forward. "Neil's been hatching his escape. Half your men are out trying to chase down Elijah. But the papers Elijah recovered from the crash site in the Amazon—which was orchestrated by Neil, by the way—prove otherwise. I have copies with me."

Elijah looked at Terrence and immediately knew how difficult this revelation was to deal with. After all, he, too, had believed in Neil. "I'm sorry, Terrence."

His boss wiped all emotion from his face, adopting a stoic expression that Elijah recognized as one of his own specialties.

"It's not your fault, Elijah. Now, with your permission, gentlemen," Terrence said, nodding to the airport officials, "we'll take our dirty linen back to Langley to sort it out."

As he turned to go, motioning for the others to bring Neil, he saw Abigail for the first time. "Who's this?"

She looked up. Elijah gave her a smile. "Abigail,

I want you to meet my boss, Terrence Roades. Terrence, this is my wife, Abigail.''

Terrence's eyes went wide. "Wife? When did this happen?"

"A lot happened since I left for the Amazon."

Turning to Abby, Terrence held out his hand. "I'm happy to meet you, Abigail. I'll be interested in hearing your story, too."

She shook his hand. "It's nice to meet you. I've enjoyed your cabin in New Mexico."

"Oh?"

"When you disappeared a couple of days ago, I gambled you'd gone to your cabin. My mistake," Elijah interjected.

"I see. Well, let's get this over." Terrence rubbed his chin. "If Neil's got anyone else on this, we want them caught before word gets out."

Abigail grabbed Elijah's arm as he started to the door. "You don't need me to tell your boss anything that happened. I want to go home. I could fly from here to Knoxville, then rent a car to get me home."

Elijah's heart contracted. He knew that it was best for Abby to go her separate way, but the knowledge didn't ease his heart. "You'll have to go with us, Abby, to Langley. To back up my story. Terrence will want to interview you, along with others. Your report on the condition of Jerry and the pilot will be important."

Her hesitation showed in her eyes. "All right, Elijah. Let's go."

"That's all, Abigail," Terrence said, closing the file before him. "You're free to go."

She gave him a puzzled look. "I'm just supposed

to walk out of here and go back to Kentucky?'' she asked.

"I'll have someone drive you to the airport. There'll be a ticket waiting for you at the airport when you arrive. And of course, ground transportation will be arranged."

She looked around the small room. "Will I get to see Elijah before I leave?"

He shook his head. "Until we understand what went on and can verify your and Elijah's story, there is to be no contact between you two."

Abigail's eyes widened.

"It's for everyone's best interest."

Standing, she took a deep breath. "I think your safety precautions could use some work, considering what's happened."

He flushed. "You're right. Still, there are rules." He stood. "I'll send someone to escort you out." Pausing at the door, he glanced back over his shoulder. "I hope we meet again, under better circumstances."

She tried to offer a polite response, but her mind remained blank. All she could do was nod.

As she waited for someone to appear, she wondered where Elijah was and what he was doing. Would he come for her, come to her mountain and seek her out, or would he convince himself that he wasn't the man of her dreams?

When a man appeared at the door, she asked, "Could I have a piece of paper and a pen? Surely, there isn't a rule against me leaving a message."

"Sure, I'll get it."

When he appeared several minutes later, he handed her what she requested. Sitting down at the table she wrote, "I don't have a red barn, but I'm willing to build one." She folded the paper and gave it to the agent. "Would you see that Elijah Kendrick receives that?"

He hesitated.

"Go ahead and read it."

The man opened the note. "I'll make sure Elijah gets this."

She prayed he would.

Elijah emerged from the interrogation room and breathed a sigh of relief. Terrence appeared in the hallway.

"You tired?" he asked Elijah.

"Yeah. How's Abigail getting along?"

"I sent her home this morning." Terrence pulled a piece of paper from his pocket and handed it to him. "She left this for you."

Opening it, Elijah read the message. She was waiting for him. Did he have the courage to claim what was his? Would it work?

"If you plan on answering that, we'd better get back to work and tie up the rest of this mess. Then you can go and see your wife."

Elijah looked up. "How do you know that's what I'm going to do?"

Terrence laughed. "You've been bitten, boy. And from the look in your eyes, you've got it bad. So do us all a favor, quit fighting it and give in."

Elijah typed the last of his report into his computer, then hit the print button. It had been a hellish ten days. They'd reviewed all the operations that Neil had compromised. It made Elijah sick to think of the number of people Neil had sold out.

Elijah was still amazed that Neil had so thoroughly betrayed his colleagues. The utter ruthlessness the man had shown shocked them all. Neil had sold his soul for money. Elijah could understand that motive, but knew he could never live with himself if he'd done the same.

He glanced down at the note Abby left him. *I don't have a red barn, but I'm willing to build one.*

She hadn't been far from his thoughts over the intervening days. He hadn't wanted to leave her as he had, but there'd been no choice.

He couldn't have gotten away from Washington for the last few days, but he could've called. So why had he avoided contacting her? Because every other person in his life whom he'd loved had left him. So if he ignored her, didn't admit he loved her, then she wouldn't leave. Right?

That didn't make sense. Wearily, he rubbed his hand over his face.

No, if he was honest with himself and looked at the monster growling at him, he could identify it for what it was. Fear. Fear because he loved her with a passion that seemed to make everything else in his past pale in comparison. Besides, he wasn't the man she pictured in her dreams.

"What are you still doing here, Elijah?" Terrence asked as he sat on the corner of the desk. "Don't you have a new wife waiting for you?"

Terrence had been tickled when he learned of Elijah's marriage and said it was just what Elijah needed.

"I knew I'd regret telling you about what happened in the jungle," he grumbled.

Laughing, Terrence shook his head. "It wouldn't have mattered, my friend. What you felt for the lady was written all over your face."

"She and I have some problems."

"Tell me, Elijah, what married couple doesn't? But it's a real treat when you work out those little bumps in the road."

Hadn't Neil said the very same thing? That he and Abby were idealists? "I don't want to quit working here."

"So don't."

"Abigail doesn't like me working here."

Terrence's brow shot up. "So work it out."

"She doesn't like working in a hospital setting."

"You're blowing a lot of smoke, Elijah." He stood. "You want the lady, and I know you'll come up with a solution to the problem."

"What about the danger? Seeing Abby with that gun jammed in her side nearly killed me."

"I've got to admit that you've got a point, but Elijah, that was an aberration. No one else I've known in the agency has lost family to a double agent. The traffic around Langley is more dangerous. No, I wouldn't trade my wife and kids for anything. They're worth it."

With the last of his fears shot down, Elijah leaned back in his chair.

Terrence reached over and took the report out of the printer. "I'm giving you a week off. Go and get your wife. And be sure and bring her by the house and introduce her to Diane. She won't believe it until she sees it."

What Terrence said made a lot of sense. He was making excuses and dancing around the issue. Since when had he turned into an ostrich? A smile broke across Elijah's face. "I think I'll just do that."

Abigail pulled up to her house and cut the engine of the car. It had felt good today to see the familiar faces of her patients at the county fair. Several people asked her where she'd gone, and she tried to explain about the trip to the Amazon.

Today's fair helped ease the sadness of missing Elijah. But it had also been torture. She had looked enviously at the couples who'd strolled the grounds with their arms around each other. She thought of the rare smiles she'd been able to coax out of her stone-faced husband. Her lower lip trembled, but she promised herself that she wasn't going to cry. Not again.

She climbed out of her car and started up the steps. She was halfway up them when she saw him, sitting in the same chair in which she'd first seen him. She stopped, unable to force air into her constricted lungs.

He stood. "Hello, Abigail." His voice was as mellow and rich as she remembered. And his face was as handsome as she'd seen in her dreams. But oddly, he appeared nervous.

As she finished coming up the steps, she tried to build up the nerve to speak. "Elijah, what are you doing here?" She sounded normal, not like someone who might fly into a million pieces. Setting down her purse on the chair, she looked at him. Her heart was pounding.

"We have some unfinished business."

She swallowed hard and waited for him to continue.

He reached into his shirt pocket and pulled out her

necklace that they had hocked in Albuquerque. "I believe this is yours."

Tears sprang to her eyes. She started to reach out, but he motioned for her to turn around. Doing so, she lifted her hair off her neck, allowing him to hook the chain.

"Thank you," she choked out.

When he was finished, he bent down and placed a soft kiss on the back of her neck. A shiver raced through her. Before she could turn around, he slipped his arms around her waist and pulled her against him.

"You've been in my thoughts every minute since we parted." He took a deep breath. "But I've been scared, Abby. You see, everyone I've ever loved has left me, so a long time ago, I decided not to give my heart. You slipped under my guard and before I knew it, I fell in love with you. I tried to ignore it. But it wouldn't go away." He softly kissed her ear. "I may not be the man you envisioned..."

His words melted the hurt she'd experienced over the last ten days. She leaned her head against his shoulder and rested her arms over his. "I love you, Elijah. You're my heart."

He turned her around and smiled down into her eyes. His fingers went to his shirt pocket again, and he brought out two simple bands. "I want this marriage to be permanent." He took the smaller band and slipped it onto her ring finger.

"It fits," she whispered in awe.

"I think I could also tell you your other measurements and be within an inch of being correct."

She blushed.

He handed her the other ring, then held out his left hand. She took the ring and slipped it on his finger.

"What are we going to do about—"

"I'd move here in a moment, Abigail, but Langley's not going to move. But there are several interesting programs in the Virginia countryside that involve midwives. I thought we might look at them. And if you're worried about the folks here, Sarah, your replacement, seemed eager to come back."

"You think you've covered all the bases, don't you, Elijah?"

His gaze became solemn. "No, but I found myself doing something very unusual as I drove up here."

"What was that?"

"I prayed."

Her lips twitched, then she laughed. "Well, your prayers have been answered. Come on inside and we'll call Sarah."

He kissed her. "Do you suppose we could call Sarah tomorrow?"

"We might wait until the day after tomorrow."

He grinned. As they approached the front door, she spotted a sack in the chair.

"What's that?" she asked.

He picked it up and handed it to her. "It's a wedding present from Dave. You remember him, our helicopter pilot?"

"Yes, I remember him." She opened the sack and pulled out a pound of Brazilian coffee beans.

"I called Dave yesterday and he flew this up here for a wedding present."

She laughed. "I can't think of a better way to start a day—waking up next to you, then having a cup of this glorious coffee."

"You're easy to please, Abigail."

"You're fixin' to find out."

They laughed and walked into the house.

Epilogue

Elijah placed his tiny baby daughter against his shoulder and gently patted her back, hoping to coax a burp from her.

"C'mon, angel," he softly whispered into her dark curls. She burped.

He grinned, then looked into her face. "You ready for the last of your bottle?"

Settling her against his chest, he gave her the bottle. He smiled down into her perfect face. He still couldn't believe that his life had turned around so dramatically. The richness of it was a miracle. He had a wife, daughter and in-laws running out his ears. His sister and Abigail's sister, and their families, had all come to their mountain home in Virginia to admire the next generation of Kendricks. Abigail had named their daughter Rachel.

"How's it going?" Abigail whispered from the doorway.

He looked up and saw her watching him. "Rachel and I had a good day. She's just about asleep now."

Abigail came into the room and looked down into her daughter's sleeping face. Elijah stood and put Rachel in her bed. His arm slipped around Abigail's waist and urged her out into the hall.

"How'd it go for you today?" he asked once they were in their room. This was her first day back to work after the birth of their daughter.

"It was good to get back to the birthing center. I can now look at the experience in a new light." She slipped her arms around his waist and rested her head on his chest. "Thank you, Elijah."

"For what?"

She leaned back in his arms. "For being the best."

"It wasn't me. It's us."

"But two halves make a whole. And I feel complete."

He hadn't thought he would ever experience that feeling, but amazingly he had. And he now knew that miracles did happen. He'd lived one.

* * * * *

Share in the joy of yuletide romance with brand-new
stories by two of the genre's most beloved writers

DIANA PALMER

and

JOAN JOHNSTON

in

LONE STAR CHRISTMAS

Diana Palmer and Joan Johnston share their favorite
Christmas anecdotes and personal stories in this
special hardbound edition.

Diana Palmer delivers an irresistible spin-off of her
LONG, TALL TEXANS series and Joan Johnston crafts an
unforgettable new chapter to **HAWK'S WAY** in this wonderful
keepsake edition celebrating the holiday season. So
perfect for gift giving, you'll want one for yourself...and
one to give to a special friend!

Available in November at your favorite retail outlet!

Only from

Silhouette ®

Look us up on-line at: http://www.romance.net   JJDPXMAS

RACHEL

CAUGHT

LEE

...in a web of danger.

Kate Devane is being
stalked on the Internet
by someone who knows
too much about her;
Connor Quinn is being
manipulated by a serial
killer. Can they trust
each other...if only to
escape the terror of a
madman's web?

A story of romantic suspense by the bestselling author of
A FATEFUL CHOICE.

Get CAUGHT this November 1997
at your favorite retail outlet.

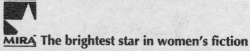

MIRA The brightest star in women's fiction

Look us up on-line at: http://www.romance.net

MRLC

The Stars of Mithra

Three gems, three beauties, three passions... the adventure of a lifetime

SILHOUETTE·INTIMATE·MOMENTS®
brings you a thrilling new series by
New York Times bestselling author

Nora Roberts

Three mystical blue diamonds place three close friends in jeopardy...and lead them to romance.

In October
HIDDEN STAR (IM#811)
Bailey James can't remember a thing, but she knows she's in big trouble. And she desperately needs private investigator Cade Parris to help her live long enough to find out just what kind.

In December
CAPTIVE STAR (IM#823)
Cynical bounty hunter Jack Dakota and spitfire M. J. O'Leary are handcuffed together and on the run from a pair of hired killers. And Jack wants to know why—but M.J.'s not talking.

In February
SECRET STAR (IM#835)
Lieutenant Seth Buchanan's murder investigation takes a strange turn when Grace Fontaine turns up alive. But as the mystery unfolds, he soon discovers the notorious heiress is the biggest mystery of all.

Available at your favorite retail outlet.

Look us up on-line at: http://www.romance.net   MITHRA

ELIZABETH AUGUST

Continues the twelve-book
series—36 HOURS—in
November 1997 with
Book Five

CINDERELLA STORY

Life was hardly a fairy tale for Nina Lindstrom. Out of work
and with an ailing child, the struggling single mom was
running low on hope. Then Alex Bennett solved her problems
with one convenient proposal: marriage. And though he had
made no promises beyond financial security, Nina couldn't
help but feel that with a little love, happily-ever-afters really
could come true!

For Alex and Nina and *all* the residents of Grand Springs,
Colorado, the storm-induced blackout was just the beginning
of 36 Hours that changed *everything!* You won't want to miss a
single book.

Look us up on-line at: http://www.romance.net   36HRS5

SILHOUETTE WOMEN KNOW ROMANCE WHEN THEY SEE IT.

And they'll see it on **ROMANCE CLASSICS**, the new 24-hour TV channel devoted to romantic movies and original programs like the special **Romantically Speaking—Harlequin™ Goes Prime Time.**

Romantically Speaking—Harlequin™ Goes Prime Time introduces you to many of your favorite romance authors in a program developed exclusively for Harlequin® and Silhouette® readers.

Watch for **Romantically Speaking—Harlequin™ Goes Prime Time** beginning in the summer of 1997.

If you're not receiving ROMANCE CLASSICS, call your local cable operator or satellite provider and ask for it today!

Escape to the network of your dreams.

See Ingrid Bergman and Gregory Peck in *Spellbound* on Romance Classics.

©1997 American Movie Classics Co. "Romance Classics" is a service mark of American Movie Classics Co. Harlequin is a trademark of Harlequin Enterprises Ltd. Silhouette is a registered trademark of Harlequin Books, S.A.

RMCLS-S-R2

Welcome to the Towers!

In January
New York Times bestselling author

takes us to the fabulous Maine coast mansion
haunted by a generations-old secret and introduces
us to the fascinating family that lives there.

Mechanic Catherine "C.C." Calhoun and hotel magnate
Trenton St. James mix like axle grease and mineral
water—until they kiss. Efficient Amanda Calhoun finds
easygoing Sloan O'Riley insufferable—and irresistible.
And they all must race to solve the mystery
surrounding a priceless hidden emerald necklace.

Catherine and Amanda

THE Calhoun Women

**A special 2-in-1 edition containing
COURTING CATHERINE and A MAN FOR AMANDA.**

Look for the next installment of
THE CALHOUN WOMEN with Lilah and Suzanna's
stories, coming in March 1998.

Available at your favorite retail outlet.

Silhouette®

Look us up on-line at: http://www.romance.net   CWVOL1

Return to the Towers!

In March
New York Times bestselling author

NORA ROBERTS

brings us to the Calhouns' fabulous
Maine coast mansion and reveals the
tragic secrets hidden there for generations.

For all his degrees, Professor Max Quartermain has a
lot to learn about love—and luscious Lilah Calhoun is
just the woman to teach him. Ex-cop Holt Bradford is
as prickly as a thornbush—until Suzanna Calhoun's
special touch makes love blossom in his heart.
And all of them are caught in the race to solve
the generations-old mystery of a priceless
lost necklace...and a timeless love.

Lilah and Suzanna
THE Calhoun Women

**A special 2-in-1 edition containing
FOR THE LOVE OF LILAH and
SUZANNA'S SURRENDER**

Available at your favorite retail outlet.

 Silhouette®

Daniel MacGregor is at it again...

New York Times bestselling author

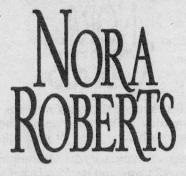

NORA ROBERTS

introduces us to a new generation of MacGregors
as the lovable patriarch of the illustrious MacGregor
clan plays matchmaker again, this time to his three
gorgeous granddaughters in

THE MACGREGOR BRIDES

From Silhouette Books

Don't miss this brand-new continuation of Nora Roberts's
enormously popular *MacGregor* miniseries.

Available November 1997 at your favorite retail outlet.

Silhouette®

Look us up on-line at: http://www.romance.net   NRMB-S